Shadows and Secrets

SHADOWS & SECRETS

Carol Blake Gerrond

AVALON BOOKS
THOMAS BOUREGY AND COMPANY, INC.
401 LAFAYETTE STREET
NEW YORK, NEW YORK 10003

© Copyright 1992 by Carol Blake Gerrond
Library of Congress Catalog Card Number: 92-73053
ISBN 0-8034-8956-0
All rights reserved.
All the characters in this book are fictitious,
and any resemblance to actual persons,
living or dead, is purely coincidental.

PRINTED IN THE UNITED STATES OF AMERICA
ON ACID-FREE PAPER
BY HADDON CRAFTSMEN, SCRANTON, PENNSYLVANIA

To all who teach—and especially the best teacher of all, my mother, Marilyn Blake.

Chapter One

It happened fast. I stepped from the bright August sun filling my new school studio into the shadowy hall. And right into Shock One!

The man was all hair—lots of it, long, coal black, and straight. He had a shaggy beard, strong, straight nose—and one green eye piercing me through a red rim. A bandage hooded the other eye.

I leaped back, darting to my right, then my left. But so did he! My soft, scared "Ohh!" exploded as his rough hand caught my forearm.

"Please—" he grated, "I didn't come here to dance!"

Before I could say a word, he'd shot around me, a well-knit figure in haggard jeans and plaid shirt. He loped down the hall with a ratty-looking garment bag slapping at his shoulder.

"Sheesh!" I whispered. I brushed a wisp from the chocolaty curls piled atop my head. A scraggly pirate wasn't part of the big plans and high hopes with which I'd started my first day as first—and only—art instructor for Sauk Valley Community Schools. But I knew what to do: Report this weirdo immediately to Mr. Jenks. Everybody in Sauk Valley agreed that Ralph Jenks was a principal par excellence. He'd know how to handle Old Blackbeard.

I hurried into the opening-day meeting. And Shock Number Two! While I'd been on the road to Illinois from a month as instructor at a Colorado art camp, Mr. Jenks had fallen and reactivated a severe back problem. He was in traction and wouldn't be back as principal for months. If at all.

Mr. Jenks had spent most of July helping me set up the new art program. Mr. Jenks had assured me that with his help, I, Mindi Carle, novice teacher, would successfully carry that program to little-bitty first-graders and all the way up to strapping high-school seniors. Now—panicky thought—Mr. Jenks was not here?

"Listen up, gang! I just got some info on the new principal."

The conference room went quiet as fiery-maned Zeta Simms, head school secretary, called us to attention.

"I haven't met Michael J. McCain," the thin, fortyish Zeta said, "but—" She ticked facts off her fingers. "He's got first-rate credentials, he's thirty-two and single, he's been an administrator in a Chicago school. And, most important, Mr. Jenks knows him well. Recommended him."

My stomach did a flip-flop. *Most important*, I worried, *he is not kind, supportive, veteran principal Mr. Jenks!*

Speculation buzzed. Why was Michael J. McCain available on such short notice? How much would a big-city man know about running a small rural school? Every voiced doubt jammed my apricot-enameled nails deeper into my fists.

"Mindi?" Lu Ann Mobley, the blond biology-chemistry teacher—and my friend from college—came to my side. She'd already taught for two years at Sauk Valley. She'd fervently urged me to come here, talking up the family atmosphere of the staff and the helpfulness of Mr. Jenks. "Wondering if you know how to teach art to kids who don't know a Picasso from a pizza?"

My tongue flicked over the tiny space between my otherwise perfect front teeth. I nodded yes. "And without Mr. Jenks—"

Lu Ann steered me firmly around a corner, away from the crowd. "Mindi, you were gutsy enough to work your way through college, even if it did take six years. You're gutsy enough to handle this job. Besides," she quipped, lightening, "once Michael J. McCain gets a load of your big brown eyes, smile that won't quit, and curves in all the right places—hey, *he'll* be helpful too!"

My return smile was a mere nervous twitch.

"Here, Min, stand in this open window and take deep breaths—" Lu Ann broke off in midsentence. "Crime-a-nently!" She peered out toward the parking lot. "Whose clunker is that in Mr. Jenks's spot?"

I followed Lu Ann's pointed finger. A blotchy brown sedan with a punched-in grill crouched among the neat compacts of Faculty Row. The misfit in the parking lot jolted my memory.

"Zeta," I called, moving to the corner, "I just remembered—"

"Can't hear you, hon," Zeta mouthed over the floor fans churning away in a desperate effort to cool the stifling air. She started toward me.

"There was a really scruffy character running loose in the hall," I said, loud with nerves. "A—a sort of a pirate—a Blackbeard! Not the kind of rowdy you'd want hanging around a schoolhouse—"

Zeta's widening eyes and sucked-in lower lip skidded me to a verbal halt. I whipped around—directly into the piercing green stare of the "pirate" himself.

"Ladies, please meet our new principal, Michael J. McCain."

Shadows and Secrets 5

In the instant of stunned silence, Mr. Whitaker, Sauk Valley's ponderous superintendent, sandwiched his bulk among Zeta, Lu Ann, and me. Beaming, he performed introductions. We all responded with appropriate sounds, but my heart was beating so fast, I couldn't hear a thing. The bandage was off a fine line of stitches above McCain's brow; now *two* fierce green eyes bored holes in me.

"Ms. Simms," Mr. Whitaker said, "would you show Mr. McCain to his office before the meeting opens?"

"Wow!" Lu Ann whispered as a startled Zeta led McCain away.

I couldn't say a word. My first day on the job, my first principal, the man who'd be evaluating my performance for the school board—and I'd already managed to insult him!

I had to move or do something horrible, like faint. I made a sudden beeline for the supply table. I scooped up a lesson-plan book, a grade book, a students' handbook, a faculty handbook—all the books and handouts necessary before one teacher could teach one second of this new school year. I scurried to a back-row seat.

Just as Lu Ann dropped into a chair beside me, a stir behind us turned us that way. Here came jowly Mr. Whitaker escorting the lean, mean Michael J. McCain to the front of the room. I whirled back, but not before I'd noticed "the pirate" was now in a handsome olive-gray suit, white shirt, and dark silk tie. Of course, he still had the beard and a head of hair Samson would have killed for. And I could tell by the uneasy rustle around me that I wasn't the only one wondering just what we had in the new principal. I was just the only one trying to scrunch lower and lower in my seat to avoid his sharp gaze.

McCain listened attentively as the staff went through the name-and-background ritual.

And then it was my turn. My throat went dry; I stood, and I wondered if everyone was noticing the way the hem of my apricot linen suit skirt was shaking. I was acutely aware of the tiny gap between my front teeth. Probably McCain scorned trembling skirts; probably he hated gaps between teeth.

I cleared my throat, and I grasped the paraphernalia in my arms as if my life depended on it. "I'm—I—" The green, level stare was focused directly on me, like a spotlight. "I'm Mindi Carle—"

And then I got a little mad. At myself as well as Old Blackbeard. What was the matter with me? I wasn't standing in front of my first-grade teacher explaining why my paper was covered with stick figures instead of "$2+2=4$." I wasn't justifying to Mom and Dad my desire to teach art instead of "something practical, like computer science."

"I'm Mindi Carle," I repeated, surprised at the calm firmness in my voice. "I'm from Rock Island, Illinois, originally, and a lot of places, including Chicago, in between—" Was that a slight squint of McCain's eyes when I said Chicago? I went on. "—in between starting college and getting my degree. But I'm finally here, and I'm glad."

I sat down to polite applause. Now McCain stood. *Relationship of parts in terms of lines and masses:* Automatically, the first law of anatomical drawing kicked in. I had to admit, Michael J. McCain's lines and masses related very well indeed. He wasn't a big man, but he was ideally proportioned. Something in his bearing—an understated confidence—made him seem taller than he actually was. And very much in control.

"Good morning." His voice was deep but scratchy. "I know you're wondering why I'm available on such short notice."

Squirms, coughs from his hearers—

"And about my somewhat rowdy—in fact, my downright *pirate-ish* appearance this morning—"

I felt the heat rising under my cheekbones.

McCain looked straight into my eyes. "To answer both questions: For several years I was vice-principal at Chicago South, in charge of discipline problems, political mix-ups—all the fun things of a big-city school. For—personal reasons, I decided to drop out for a while. The past two years, I've been up in Minnesota, guiding hunters and fishermen."

"That explains the excess hair," Lu Ann whispered.

"But not why he went there in the first place," I countered stubbornly, glad to break with McCain's glance.

"I intended to get civilized before today's meeting," McCain was saying. "I didn't count on my Ford Bronco getting creamed from behind last night on the way here. By the time I got stitched up and found a Rent-a-Wreck, it was almost midnight. So, bear with me, please. And quick, somebody tell me—where's the nearest barber?"

Laughter spurted from every corner of the room. There was one cold zone in the improving climate. Me.

"If you're wondering how I'll do in a system of four hundred students, K through 12, when I'm used to five times that many, and all high schoolers, all I can say is—I'm wondering too."

This ready admission of fallibility lured the rest of the staff even further into McCain's camp.

"I won't be trying to replace Ralph Jenks," McCain went on. "Nobody could. But he's told me that in this system everyone works together yet carries his own weight. So if we all keep handling things that way, we'll justify his faith. In all of us." He took his seat.

"Let's win one for the Gipper!" I muttered sarcastically.

"I don't think this man talks in clichés," Lu Ann murmured.

I didn't argue with her. Nor did I change my opinion of Old Blackbeard. I just made up my mind to stay as far away from him and his mean green eyes as I could.

Just as Mr. Whitaker was about to fire us up with further inspiration, McCain stepped back to the podium. "I almost forgot. Mrs. Jenks lined me up with some temporary housing until I can find an apartment. If you need to get in touch with me outside school hours, my address is—" He drew a slip of paper from his coat pocket. "One hundred North Kellor Avenue."

One hundred North Kellor Avenue. It took a second for the digits to penetrate my seething brain. Suddenly the armload of books and manuals I'd accumulated this morning on my way to becoming a teacher hit the floor with a resounding *splat!*

"One hundred North Kellor?" I gasped, sitting bolt upright. "But—that's where *I* live!"

Chapter Two

"**I** have *never* been so embarrassed in my life!" I slung my suitcase onto the antique cherry four-poster.

"Hey! Watch it!" Lu Ann, perched on the edge of the bed, lunged sideways.

"Oh. Sorry." I plopped on the other side of the suitcase. "But the snickers, the smirks when everybody realized Blackbeard and I were going to be living together—I mean, well—you know what I mean!"

"Sure, Min, sure," Lu Ann soothed through a giggle. "But it was funny. Especially the surprise on Blackbeard's face."

"Glad we could provide a little comedy relief."

Lu Ann smothered her grin. "Don't get hyper, Min. Anybody who ever had Miss Marie Kellor for a social-studies teacher—and I guess that's about half the two thousand good citizens of this town—knows there'd be no hanky-panky going on under her roof.''

"Oh, I suppose you're right," I agreed after consideration. "But when I stayed here in July, Miss Kellor said she never took in more than one 'paying guest,' as she calls me, at a time."

"Heaven knows there's plenty of space in this old mini-palace." Lu Ann slipped off the bed to wander around, inspecting the faded elegance of my two big rooms. "She could house half a dozen teachers if she wanted to."

"Oh, space isn't the problem; besides Miss Kellor's bedroom downstairs, there are five more on this floor. Not to mention a full-sized attic and a cupola on top! So—where does she decide to put Old Blackbeard?"

"From the worry lines on your face, I'd guess close by?"

"Here's the note she left me. 'Mindi, dear—I'll be at the Friday Bridge Club this afternoon. If Mr. McCain gets here before I return, would you please show him up to Brother Nathan's quarters? Thanks, M.K.' Thank goodness, she's back, so she can show him the room herself." I crumpled the note into a ball. "She's putting him right across the hall."

"Wait a minute," Lu Ann protested. "You lost me. Who's this Brother Nathan?"

I hopped off the bed to pace over the soft Oriental

rug. "Nathan was Miss Kellor's brother. He died nearly ten years ago." I stopped beside the cozy love seat angled out from the marble fireplace. "According to Zeta—"

"Ahh, The Gospel According to Zeta—"

I ignored the tongue-in-cheek interruption. "According to Zeta, Nathan Kellor is the reason Miss Kellor has to take in 'paying guests.' Seems the Kellors used to be the wealthiest family in Sauk Valley, until Brother Nathan got his hands on the family fortune. Zeta says he was a real good-timer—blew just about every cent, leaving his sister with a run-down hunting lodge, her teacher's pension, and this house."

Lu Ann fingered the long handmade lace curtains floating soft and stately in the floor-to-ceiling bay window. "Kellor House is so beautiful. Antique red brick, great arched windows—you know about architecture, Mindi. What style is this house?"

"Italianate. With touches of mid-nineteenth-century Americana."

"It's one classy joint," Lu Ann mused.

"I agree," I said, forgetting my immediate problem for the moment. "At first I felt bad because I was too broke to get an apartment. Then in July I met Miss Kellor. And the house. Both of them gracious and good smelling and—accepting. I've been looking forward to a real home here."

And now it's going to be spoiled by that—that disrupter, Michael J. McCain, I added mentally.

Aloud, I said, "Zeta told me Miss Kellor adored Brother Nathan; he was her one blind spot. I can't believe she's letting Old Blackbeard profane Nathan Kellor's sacred shrine."

Lu Ann's china-blue eyes regarded me quizzically.

"Come on," I urged, "I'll show you what I mean."

Lu Ann didn't need coaxing to follow me across the broad center hall. I threw open a massive door to two interconnecting rooms, the first an office.

"Shades of Teddy Roosevelt!" Lu Ann stepped wonderingly into the rich, all-male ambience of Nathan Kellor's world. The main business conducted from this office was evident: Mounted game fish, heads of deer, moose, and elk—even a stuffed Siberian wolf and an African lion—lined the walls. Leather furniture clustered around a stone fireplace framed by guns and photographs of hunting parties.

"Not too hard to see why Kellor went broke, is it?" I said.

"Wow! I've got a feeling this is a little ritzier setup than Michael J. McCain had in Minnesota," Lu Ann ventured.

I tapped a nervous forefinger against my bottom lip. "Lu Ann, what was he doing up in the North Woods the past two years? At thirty, who just 'drops out' of a profession? Who that's any good at it, anyway."

Lu Ann considered. "It does seem odd. Still, you hear teachers say, after a bad day, that they'd like to take the next slow boat to China! And inner-city schools can be combat zones."

"But he said he dropped out for personal reasons, not professional."

"Whatever the reason, it must be too painful to talk about."

"Or too damaging."

"But Mr. Jenks thinks well of him." Lu Ann shrugged thoughtfully and started to leave. "By the way, Min, want to go speed walking tomorrow morning before it gets too hot?"

"Sure," I agreed. "And thanks for helping me unpack my car."

"No problem," she said, waving off my thanks.

I was glad Lu Ann was my friend. She was one of the prettiest women I knew, inside and out. She had a natural confidence and optimistic outlook I sometimes had to work at.

After she left, I got out of my hot school clothes and into my coolest sundress. I bathed my face in cool water, and then I started down the back staircase—the one used by servants in the glory days of Kellor House—on my way to the kitchen. Miss Kellor had come home a while ago and called up to me to help myself to lemonade in the fridge. A rumble, as of a car in its death throes, stopped me cold. McCain!

I scrambled on down to the kitchen and ran to the windows overlooking the backyard. Sure enough, McCain's rented monstrosity came lumbering along the curving drive that separated Kellor House from its plainer neighbors. And there was Miss Marie Kellor in her second-best pink crepe dress and her gardening gloves, smoothing her snowy-white hair and greeting the pirate-principal as cordially as if she took in Blackbeards every day of the week.

I whisked away from the window. *I'll get my cold drink and get out of here,* I told myself. *No way am I sticking around to be cannon fodder for McCain's killer stares.*

I reached into a cupboard for a cut-glass tumbler. Miss Kellor might be poor, but she was genteel poor; nothing of her heirloom china, silver, or glassware was too good for her "guests'" use. It was just one of her generosities of spirit I loved. Another reason to hate McCain's glary intrusion into a warm, harmonious home.

"Mindi?" That was Miss Kellor calling from the screened porch that ran across the back of the house.

For a second I considered fleeing up the back stairs without answering, but I could hear footsteps already in the central hall.

"In the kitchen," I replied. I yanked open the fridge and grabbed an etched-glass pitcher of lemonade—real lemonade with seeds in it. I felt McCain's presence

Shadows and Secrets 17

even with my back turned. My grip tightened on the glass tumbler. *This is my territory*, I reminded myself. *I got to Kellor House first; I made friends with Miss Kellor first. And I'll be here after he's gone.*

"Mindi—" Miss Kellor's plump little person, firm in its ever-present Spandex foundation, was at my elbow. "Mr. McCain is here. Of course, you two have already met."

"Of course," I answered stiffly, without turning. A cross between a cough and a "yes" scratched from McCain.

"Well, then, if you'd take Mr. McCain up to his rooms, I'll start getting us an early dinner—"

McCain stopped her with, "Miss Kellor, thank you very much, but if you'll just point me in the right direction, I'll find my own way."

I didn't like the curt brush-off. I'd just poured my lemonade; I swung around with the intention of putting him at unease with a long, cool stare over the rim of my glass. The lemonade halted halfway to my lips.

He looked so hot and tired. His hair was shaggier, his eyes redder-rimmed than they'd been this morning. There was no missing the fatigued slump of his well-developed shoulders.

Suddenly I recalled the time my car was broadsided, how every muscle in my body ached from the jolt even though technically I was unhurt. I remembered standing for hours under a pummeling shower to relieve the pain. And I knew that if the shower head in Nathan's—now McCain's—bathroom was as limed up as the one in mine, it had all the force of a wet noodle.

"Here." On pure impulse I thrust the lemonade toward the exhausted principal. *I can treat him like the jerk he is tomorrow,* I promised myself, *when he's not dead on his feet.*

He looked doubting for a second, as if he suspected sabotage; then the shadowed lines around his eyes softened a little.

"Thanks. I can sure use a cold drink."

My empty hand retreated to my side, strangely livened by the brush against his. As an artist I saw hands as nearly as expressive of human character and feeling as the face. His were callused, and the knuckles properly square and masculine. Yet the long, tanned fingers tapered slightly, with an upward tilt at the tips. Sensitive hands.

McCain downed the icy beverage in one long swig and set the empty glass on the counter. "Thank you, Ms. Carle. I've never tasted anything better."

He turned to Miss Kellor. "If you don't mind, I'm going to skip dinner tonight. I just want to get a shower and then crash—for about twenty-four hours!"

"I can understand, Michael," Miss Kellor assured him. "Zeta Simms called this morning to tell me you'd arrived after considerable difficulty."

I saw the irony flash in McCain's weary expression.

Shadows and Secrets   19

"Yes," he said in a gravelly tone. "I think I can count on Ms. Simms to keep the news rolling, can't I?"

Miss Kellor's laugh was guarded. "You can, but she—like everyone Ralph Jenks chooses—is excellent in her job. I've never heard her knowingly pass any—hurtful—information."

It had to be my imagination. Miss Kellor's eyebrow lift wasn't really cautionary. Was it?

McCain's expression tightened; then he tipped his head in a nod and picked up his battered garment bag. "Do I take the stairs I saw as we came in through the hall?"

"Oh—yes! Mindi, would you mind?"

All the way up the grand walnut spiral leading to the second floor, I puzzled. Something strange was going on here. Miss Kellor had as much as said, "If Zeta discovers your secret, Michael, she'll keep it." *What* secret?

I led McCain into Nathan Kellor's suite. His response was, for such a seemingly tough-hided man, boyish.

"*Ho*-ly To-*le*-do!" He set down his luggage and pivoted to take in the wonders of the office. He prowled into the bedroom, then came back to face me. "This is a whole lot more than I expected for what I'm paying! And meals come with it?"

"Yes. But we take turns cooking. There are a couple of restaurants in town, if you'd rather eat there."

A smile flickered over his tired face. "Restaurant food gets boring in a hurry. Besides, I can cook too. Sort of."

He strolled to the gun cabinets standing beside the fireplace. They opened easily enough; the keys were already inserted.

"Is everybody in this town so trusting of strangers?"

I didn't like the almost accusatory tone. "I don't know; I'm not a native, either."

He removed one massive rifle. "That's right," he commented with an almost too-casual inspection of the gun, "you've been in lots of places, haven't you? Rock Island, Chicago...."

Uneasiness sifted through me. Who was this man? I didn't know him; maybe *Mr. Jenks* didn't know him as well as he thought he did. And here he stood with a gun in his hand... right across the hall from my room....

"Ms. Carle, I don't intend to 'waste' you."

The quiet irony in his gratey tones sent the blood flaming into my cheeks. "I didn't think you would," I flared.

"No?" McCain stepped closer, frowning. "Every time I've turned around today, there you are, glaring at me like I'm Jack the Ripper. Just who *do* you think I am?"

Of all the nerve! He stood there frowning at *me,* as if *I* were the one— "For crying out loud!" I blurted.

Shadows and Secrets

"You *do* look like Jack the Ripper! Hiding out behind all that hair—all those green eyes with scorched red lids—"

"*Two* eyes," he blasted back. "There were only two the last time I looked, and they're red because I haven't had any sleep for thirty-six hours! The only thing I'm hiding from behind the hair and beard is the Minnesota mosquitoes! They'll eat you alive if you don't keep your skin covered!"

We exchanged mutual furious scowls. Then I wheeled and headed for the door, only to find it blocked by McCain's vigorous body. "Let me out, *sir*," I ground out through set teeth.

"Listen," he said, tight-mouthed. "Listen—uh—" He drew a long breath. "That lemonade you gave me—that was the nicest thing that's happened to me lately. Thanks. A lot."

All right. So he wasn't a *complete* jerk....

Chapter Three

*H*ow *the heck did I get into this ridiculous situation?*
 I knew, of course, exactly why I stood in the carriage-house loft in my peach shorts and scooped-neck tank top, shivering in the early-morning chill. It all happened because just as Michael sat down to breakfast, he'd gotten a call to meet with Harley Dikes, the school-board president, at nine. Immediately he'd found that Sauk Valley's only barber had chosen this Saturday, of all days, to leave town.
 And that's when Miss Kellor got into the act. "Oh, dear, Michael," she'd piped up, "maybe I could get you in to one of the local beauticians. Although they're usually booked solid on Saturday mornings...."
 "Please!" Michael had thrown up a warning hand.

"I don't want to make my first enemy in Sauk Valley by bumping some lady out of her weekly hair appointment!"

"But Harley Dikes is a difficult man at best," Miss Kellor had persisted. "You wouldn't want your first meeting with him to be—uh—handicapped—by lack of a haircut. Now, who could we get?"

Oh, no, Miss Kellor, let's not handicap Michael, I fumed. *Let's put Mindi on the spot. Let's open our pretty little mouth and say,* "Mindi—remember, dear, in July you styled my hair? Everybody says it's the best cut I've had in years!"

And then, I recalled, *I said all the right things—* "But I've only cut permed hair—I've never done a man's hair—blah, blah, blah—" *For all the good it did me. Now, where are those danged scissors?*

I couldn't stay mad at Miss Kellor, of course. Not after she'd given me what used to be Nathan Kellor's party room for my own private studio. Last night I'd vacuumed ten years' dust from this loft, then carried up my collection of canvasses and art supplies. About all that remained from Brother Nathan's heady times were a couple of stools, an old chest, and a Franklin stove that made bearable an Illinois winter. But the natural lighting was good, pouring in through skylights as easily as rain came through the north end of the roof.

"Ah, here they are." I clashed the pair of keen

scissors I extracted from a box of art tools. If only I could just cut the troubling Michael J. McCain right out of my life—

"I hope that's not my ears you're shearing!"

The arrestingly husky voice spun me toward the stairs. "I didn't hear—"

My breathless exclamation broke off as I looked into Michael's face; my lips started to twitch.

"They say everything looks better in the morning, but I'm not so sure."

I fought back a giggle. Where his heavy beard had been fifteen minutes ago, now shone bare skin, at least three shades lighter than the rest of his tanned face. The only things whiter were his teeth gleaming in an uneven grin. He ran a hand over his well-defined jaw.

"From Blackbeard to Frankenstein in twelve easy razor strokes. And I was trying to get *less* scary."

"Oh—uh—you don't look—scary—uh—" Words failed. What he looked was comical. It was too much; I couldn't stop the laughter that bubbled up and out the tiny front-tooth gap I was sure he wouldn't like. "I'm sorry," I apologized. "I shouldn't laugh."

"Go ahead. A lot of Minnesota mosquitoes are yukking their heads off!"

The difference between Michael J. McCain exhausted and the same man rested and chipper was astonishing. The green of his eyes, so threatening yesterday, sparkled now like seawater in the morning light. His smile was guarded but friendly.

"I, uh, realize this is an imposition. Especially since I was pretty—testy—with you yesterday. So, if you'd rather not—"

He glanced at the scissors gleaming in my hand.

He's afraid I'll give him a Mohawk, I gloated. "It's up to you." I toyed, nonchalant, with the scissors. "Miss Kellor is right, though, about Harley Dikes."

"What's his problem?"

"Oh, you know," I threw off, "how some people are when they get a little authority."

Michael's smile turned suspicious. "*How* are they?"

I looked him directly in the eye. "Supersensitive. Quick to take offense over—perceived—insults."

Michael's jaw pulled awry. "I take your point, Ms. Carle." His hands rested on his narrow hips. "Look, we got off to a bad start yesterday. But I took a gander at myself last night before I dropped into bed, and I agree—I looked like Captain Hook on his worst day."

I nodded yes.

"But, on the other hand, you seem more than unhappy that I've come to Sauk Valley. Especially to Miss Kellor's."

"That's not so," I hedged, aware he was right on top of the truth. "But—I—I—" I decided to go with a fact or two. "I'm edgy too. About my first teaching year, about Mr. Jenks not being here to help me get this brand-new program off the ground. And, frankly—"

Oh, boy, should I tell him what bothered me most of all? I summoned a deep breath. "Frankly, I didn't expect my boss to be looking over my shoulder twenty-four hours a day. Living here, right across the hall."

Michael's hands lifted in a gesture of sweet reason. "I won't be here long. As soon as I have a minute, I'll find an apartment. Meanwhile, let's work it out this way: At school, I'm your boss; here, I'm just—Miss Kellor's other 'guest.'"

I must have looked doubting.

Something flashed in his eyes. "Listen—if you want me to buzz off, just say so!" He turned to leave, an angry hitch in his shoulders.

"Wait—" I hadn't meant to insult him. Again. I pulled a stool into the best light. "You really can't meet Mr. Dikes with that hair. He's—conservative, to say the least." I gestured to a stool. "Take a seat. Please?"

Michael regarded me skeptically for a second. Then his smile returned. "Okay. But—" He glanced pointedly at the scissors in my hand. "You realize this is an act of faith on my part, Ms. Carle?"

I laughed. "Mindi," I corrected. "Remember? Equal rights here at Miss Kellor's."

He settled on the stool. "Mindi. I think I read Mindora on the roster of faculty names?"

"Ugh!" The expression leaped out of me. "My parents named me for a rich great-aunt. Then she died and left everything to her cat!"

Michael laughed. "Lucky feline! Well, I like Mindi, anyway."

And I liked the way his throaty tones touched the nickname.

I'd brought a towel to put around his shoulders, but Michael had exchanged the knit pullover and cutoffs he'd had on at breakfast for a crisp multistriped business shirt and dress pants. As I surveyed the mass of hair to be removed, I suggested maybe he'd like to take off his shirt. "Otherwise you'll be itching all through your meeting with Mr. Dikes."

After a second's hesitation he rose from the stool and followed my suggestion. "I suppose it's presumptuous of me to ask where you learned to cut hair?"

I laughed softly. "Oh, one of the many odd jobs I took to pay my way through college was shampooer in a posh salon. I picked up styling tips watching Mr. Ricky himself."

"Mr. *Ricky?* Hey, now!" he kidded.

He draped the towel around his hard, powerful shoulders and started back to the stool. Suddenly he noticed a pile of portrait sketches I'd set on an easel. I saw his quick, nearly imperceptible double take. He stopped by the easel, riffled through the portraits.

"These sketches—they look like courtroom illustrations, the kind you see in the newspaper? Or on TV?"

"They are."

There it was—a fine line of tension tightening his jaw. "You—uh—you've been part of the court scene?"

"Briefly. When I was studying portraiture at the Art Institute in Chicago, I filled in for a court illustrator who had emergency surgery."

His fingers tensed on a sketch he was holding. "Really? Did you get into some interesting cases?"

I laughed, not really amused. "I was needed for only one case—a celebrity fest. You probably heard about it, even up in the North Woods. Kane vs. Kane."

It wasn't my imagination; when I mentioned the last year's "beautiful people" divorce case of two rich, spoiled Chicagoans, the tension slid out of his jaw as stealthily as it had crept in.

He glanced at the sketch in his hand. "I'm always amazed at what artists can say about a person with a few pencil or brush strokes. I couldn't do it in a million years."

"It's all a matter of lines and masses, lights and shadows," I explained. "And it's what I love to do."

"You're not into sunsets and picturesque horizons, then?" he inquired lightly.

"They're fine. But for as long as I can remember,

it's been human faces—human personalities—that have fascinated me."

He nodded thoughtfully. Then he snapped a glance at his watch. "Uh-oh—we'd better get a move on!"

"Right." He sat on the stool, and I divided his black mane into manageable portions. It was clean, crisp, and smelling of good shampoo.

"Okay." I wet my lips. "Here we go!"

For the next few minutes the only sound was the snick of blades severing sheaves of hair. Just as the lack of conversation got really noticeable, we both spoke at once.

"How did you—"

"So Mr. Dikes is—"

Michael laughed. "Ladies first," he insisted.

"I was just going to ask, how did you get acquainted with Mr. Jenks?"

"The hard way." Michael chuckled. "He was teaching math at Chicago South when I hit high school all set to be cock of the walk."

"And?" I paused in the middle of a snip.

"And he got me in line. In fact—" Michael paused. "If it hadn't been for him, I'd probably have been another dead punk in the Chicago streets long ago."

"What was his secret?" If there were any shortcuts to managing difficult students, I definitely wanted to know them.

Michael looked up at me, intent. "No secret. I just

grew to respect him because he respected me. Enough to insist that I behave and that I learn. No excuses because I came from a bad situation. But the next summer, he and Mrs. Jenks took a bunch of us junior-grade hoods up to Minnesota for our own private camp. All the boating and fishing we could handle, as long as we worked with the Jenkses on our worst school subjects one solid hour every day—"

Michael came to an abrupt halt. His jaw clamped to hold down some deep feeling.

"Ralph Jenks turned my life around," he said, and there was a little more gravel in his naturally husky voice. "So I wouldn't refuse a request for help from him if it killed me. So—" He shifted deliberately to a less serious mood. "Mr. Harley Dikes, fearless leader of the Sauk Valley school board—he's pretty hard-nosed?"

I resumed snipping. "Well, I can tell you that the day I was hired, he lost no time letting me know both art and I were coming into the system practically over his dead body. Art was 'a waste of money,' and I was 'too inexperienced' to develop and carry out a whole new program."

Michael chuckled. "That must have been a real upper!"

"Um-hum," I murmured. "But I'd run into opposition to my teaching plans before."

He gave me a questioning glance.

"Mom and Dad. They were planning more for retirement than a baby when I finally came along. They always felt art was a pretty chancy teaching field." I remembered with pain the only really fierce argument I'd ever had with my parents. "So they—uh—kind of gave me an ultimatum: Go into something 'practical' or finance my own way through college."

Michael didn't say anything for a second. Then, "Did you become an art teacher to spite them? Or because you really wanted to?"

It was a fair-enough question and one I'd asked myself a few times. And I knew my answer. "I want to teach art. I've wanted to ever since my first art teacher said I drew the best faces she'd ever seen from a third-grader. And I don't waste my energies on spite."

He nodded thoughtfully. "That's a good attitude, Mindi. For your career, or any other part of your life."

I liked hearing that.

I resumed the haircut, moving around Michael in a circle as I shaped his black hair around a classically structured head. I liked his good-natured smile, his easy humor. I liked his admiration for Mr. Jenks. And the fact that he was a very attractive man—even with a stitched forehead and a two-toned face—that wasn't lost on me, either.

I stood directly in front of him, checking the haircut for balance, then leaned forward to clip a straggler at the crown. His breath was warm—and suddenly unsteady—at our momentary closeness. I drew back quickly. But I couldn't say I was displeased that he wasn't immune to me, either.

"Just a little touch with the brush," I murmured, "and—voilà!" I handed him a mirror from my equipment basket.

A faintly exaggerated pulse throbbed in his neck as he studied his reflection. His half laugh seemed a bit self-conscious. "Mr. Ricky couldn't have done better."

"Min-n-di? Ready to go walking?"

Michael and I both turned quickly toward Lu Ann's musical yodel emanating from the stairs. The towel dropped from Michael's shoulders. Swiftly he began buttoning himself into his shirt. But not before I'd noticed a dark-red scar on his back, riding along the lower left edge of his rib cage.

Lu Ann popped into the loft, pert as a daisy in her soft yellow jersey playsuit.

"Oh! I didn't know—I can come back—" she stammered, looking from my slightly flushed face to Michael's unnaturally white one.

"That's all right. I'm on my way out," he said, brushing a quick hand over his newly shorn locks. "Thanks again," he threw at me and practically ran for the staircase.

Lu Ann's slow, impish grin got to me. "It's all

perfectly harmless, and don't jump to any conclusions!" I warned her.

"Did I say anything?" she mocked with an oh-so-artless shrug. "Maybe it's the new thing for principals to run around with their shirttails out. And the front all misbuttoned!"

That night when I went up to bed, a small, luxuriously wrapped package stood before my door. I slipped off the glamorous paper; inside was a bottle of my favorite scent, the one I'd been wearing that morning, and a note: *The haircut—and the advice about Mr. D.—both right on the money. Mike.*

Chapter Four

"Mith Carle, I'm all thtuck with *featherth*!"

"Niki—how in the world—"

It was Friday, and my teaching career was exactly four weeks old. I bobbed from one imminent disaster to another as twenty-five first-graders ended the day deep in the creation of "magic eyeglasses, a project to develop cutting and design skills." Well, that's how I'd written it up in July under "Daily Objectives," anyway.

"Class," I called over the incredible hubbub, "we'll finish our glasses next week. Just put them on the project table as you leave the room."

"But I wanna take mine home!"

"Sorry, Justin. Kurt, get those scissors out of Brandon's hair."

"Pwease, Miss Carle, I want to show Mom—"

"We don't want to miss our bus, do we, Johnny? Let's get everything all cleaned up, and I'll see you Monday."

Five minutes later the mini-Gauguins were gone and I was collapsed on a pint-sized wooden chair in a room awash in feathers, tagboard, and stray glitter.

"Hi, kiddo; how's it going?" Zeta breezed in and clapped a pair of tagboard "glasses" to her temples.

My eyes rolled despairingly. "Zeta, if you *ever* again see me enter this school with anything remotely resembling feathers, call for the men in white coats!"

"Rough day, huh?" Zeta commented, sympathetic. "By the way, Head Honcho's on his way over." The gangly secretary began an efficient neatening of the clutter atop the project table.

"Oh, shoot! I'd better get this room spiffed up!" I jumped into action, thankful for Zeta's warning. I didn't intend to have Michael find me goofing off.

Not after the past four weeks I'd just put in. The well-drawn lesson plans I'd worked on every spare minute last summer—how did I so thoroughly miscalculate the time element? The hundred-and-one interruptions that turned so many days into a shambles? Why didn't Mr. Jenks warn me that I'd go home every night feeling as if I'd been put through a wringer? That

Shadows and Secrets

I'd lose ten pounds and tear around all day with a knot in the pit of my stomach?

"Zeta," I inquired while hurriedly straightening chairs, "what do you think of Mr. McCain after working with him for a month?"

"I like him," she said without hesitation. "I know he thought at first I was some kind of flake. But since he's found how many different hats a small-school principal has to wear, he's not too proud to ask me how things are done." She stopped to summarize. "I'd say he's fair, square, and—misses no signals." Her gaze at me sharpened. "What do *you* think of your first principal—and current housemate?"

"Oh." She'd taken me by surprise. "He's—fine. In both roles. But—" I paused long enough to pull off a piece of tagboard glued to my shoe sole. "For someone who misses no signals, he doesn't give off many of his own, does he? I mean—about his past."

A wry grin teased Zeta's mobile features. "No, and his low-key way of deflecting questions makes it tough for me to pry."

A familiar male tone cut across our talk. "Could I see you for a minute, Ms. Carle?"

Michael's voice had lost the raspiness of our first-time meeting, but it still generated a certain anxiety in me. As he'd suggested that morning in the loft at Kellor House—during the rare time he was there instead of attending to school matters—we were on more or less casual terms. But at school—ah .... At school I never forgot for a minute that *Mr.* McCain was the principal, the first and most influential link in the chain of command that would decide my fitness as a teacher—and therefore, my future.

I pasted on a smile. "Yes, of course, Mr. McCain."

The color in his face had evened to a healthy light bronze; the subtle teal thread in his navy-blue sport coat was the perfect emphasis to his sea-green eyes and thick ebony hair. As he took a seat on the corner of the teacher's desk, he looked a far cry from a scruffy pirate.

"I'll be buzzing along," Zeta offered diplomatically and left.

Michael, with an amused slant to his jaw, watched the supercharged secretary barge out the door. He turned to me, pleasant but businesslike. "So. How are things going?"

"Oh—fine. Just fine," I lied. Admit to him I spent a lot of time floundering? No way.

"Good. I'm setting up a schedule of class visitations—the mandatory teacher-evaluation procedure, you know—and I'd like to get to you next week."

My heart started thudding. I'd known this was coming, but it still scared me. "Yes—when?"

Michael consulted the class schedule in his hand. "Let's see.... How about Thursday, seventh period? Art History One?" He looked up at me expectantly.

Shadows and Secrets 39

My heart struck rock bottom. The single most troublesome class of my day. The problem was a senior, Lonnel Dikes, the Elvis lookalike son of board president Harley Dikes. Considering Mr. Dikes's attitude toward art, I assumed son Lonny would never darken the door to one of my classes. Wrong! Lonny, whom I suspected practiced his lady-killing Elvis leers in front of a mirror, had turned up in Art History I, determined to be a self-injected thorn in my side. He had a way of pushing me to the brink with his cagey impudence, then backing off the instant before he passed the point of no return. After trying every "behavioral modification strategy" in the book, plus some plain commonsense tactics of my own, I was fed up with Lonny Dikes.

"You—uh—you'd prefer I'd visit some other hour?"

He knows something's wrong, I worried. "Well—no. Seventh hour Thursday is fine." *"Sauk Valley teachers carry their own weight."* I remembered Michael's words to the faculty that first day of school. He must have handled some hard-core problems in Chicago. Wouldn't he consider me a wimp if I couldn't solve a situation with a less-than-lethal kid like Lonny Dikes?

"Okay, if you're sure," Michael said, still eyeing me carefully.

"It really doesn't matter what class you visit," I

bluffed over my qualms. "We're moving right along in each of them." I clutched at a feather sailing by and stuffed it into my pocket.

His smile was dry. "I'm glad to hear that." He reached out to pick a bit of tagboard from the French braid keeping my hair off my neck in the lingering September warmth.

Self-consciously I swept a quick hand over the braid. "Things get a little messy when you introduce first-graders to shape and texture," I commented too brightly. I whisked a sprinkle of glitter off the desk top and into my palm.

"I'm sure." Still smiling, Michael rose to leave. "Thursday, then, seventh period."

I watched him go; then I let out the breath I'd been holding. Oh, boy!

The moment had arrived: E-Day. Thursday, seventh hour, Art History I. With Michael sitting at the back of the school studio, I launched a discussion of the history of sculptured portraiture. Lonny Dikes had his usual front-row perch; he sat attentive and taking notes, for all the world a model student. With his back to Michael, he was free to heckle me with smart looks and sly smiles.

When—and how—is he going to strike? I worried.

In spite of my nervousness I was determined to carry through my carefully developed lesson plan. I picked

Shadows and Secrets 41

up a volume of color plates to illustrate the difference between the rigid stylization of early Egyptian sculpture and the astonishing realism of the late-nineteenth-century European masters.

"Here," I said, showing a plate of the "Colossi of Memmnon," "you see how the seated figures of the pharaohs conform to the rectangular shape of the stones. The human proportions are truthful, yet there's no feeling of personality to the figures.

"On the other hand," I continued, preparing to open the heavy volume at the next spot I'd marked, "around the turn of this century, you have Auguste Rodin creating statues so full of life, he was accused of using molds of actual human bodies. For instance—" I flipped the book open. "In 'The Burghers of Calais,' you can practically *feel* the energy, the passion—"

There was a sharp intake of somebody's breath, then a flurry of embarrassed titters. I snapped a look at the page I was showing. Someone had moved the bookmark! Instead of the dignified—and fully clothed—"Burghers of Calais," I was exposing Rodin's gracefully erotic naked lovers in "The Kiss." Someone had stuck a cutout of a beer can on the base of the sculpture, and a title composed from magazine print: *In Conference: Do Not Disturb*. But the crowning touch was the names pasted to the figures: *McCain and Ms. Carle*.

Later I couldn't believe I'd had the presence of mind to coolly turn the page to "The Burghers" and continue my presentation. I didn't dare look at Michael. Somehow my mouth produced the right words even as my brain reeled with embarrassment. And suspicion.

Lonnel Dikes. I knew as surely as I stood there he was behind this scummy little prank.

I got to the end of the period knowing the students hadn't heard a word I'd said after they'd glimpsed the doctored illustration. When the bell finally rang, they gathered their books and fled the room as if it were on fire. I heard their outbursts of giggles and nervous exclamations as they escaped down the hall.

As Lonny started past me, a lopsided Elvis grin giving away his satisfaction, I stopped him. "I'll see you immediately after school, Lonnel," I hissed barely above a whisper.

"Can't, Ms. Carle. Football practice." He lounged out of the room, an arrogant pup.

Mercifully Michael waited until the room emptied before he came forward slowly to where I stood battling tears of angry frustration. "May I see the book?" he asked softly.

Without a word I handed him the volume.

He opened it to the offending page. He chuckled grimly. "Any idea who our locker-room artist is?"

"I can't prove anything, but—yes. I think it's Lonny Dikes."

"Your reasons?"

I told Michael about the ongoing struggle I'd had

Shadows and Secrets 43

with Lonny. "Just now I told Lonny to come see me after school. He said he couldn't miss football practice."

From the fiery flash in Michael's green eyes, I knew somebody—besides me—was going to wish this day had gone differently. "Come to my office after school. Don't worry. Master Lonnel Dikes will be there."

I felt terrible; I wanted to cry. The tardy bell jangled. "Oh, gosh—I'm late for my first-grade class."

"Listen—" Michael's gruff voice was compassionate. "You handled that classroom flap really well. Why don't you take this last period off, get hold of yourself."

"No." I wanted to crawl into a corner and bawl my eyes out. Instead, I straightened; my jaw firmed. "Thank you very much, but I have a class to teach. If you'll excuse me—"

Hardly aware of what I was doing, I found the packet of materials I needed for my first-graders and walked resolutely out the door. I glanced back; I saw Michael's slow nod of approval.

"My boy is going to miss the most important football game of the year because some incompetent little *art* teacher can't take a joke? An *art* teacher?" Harley Dikes's bellow echoed off the Kellor House back porch. "I want an end to this nonsense right now!"

"Mr. Dikes—" Michael stepped from the hallway

onto the porch. "I'm not in the habit of discussing school business outside my office. If you'll come in tomorrow morning—"

"No!" Dikes's beefy face shoved close to Michael's calm one. "We'll have it out now! What do you think you're doing, giving my boy a one-day suspension for tomorrow? I want him out of that silly class and into something practical—something *important*—as of morning. And I want him on that football field tomorrow night!"

I came up behind Michael, followed by a mystified Miss Kellor, who knew nothing of the brouhaha sizzling at school. I didn't have to look at Michael's face to know the iron response Dikes would arouse with those demands.

"For heaven's sake, Harley, lower your voice so the whole neighborhood doesn't hear you!" Miss Kellor commanded, stepping around to face him.

Dikes bit back some uncouth expression, temporarily abashed by his schoolboy respect for this small woman who'd once been the kindly but undisputed mistress of her classroom.

"Sorry, Miss Kellor," he rasped, "but this really doesn't concern you."

"It most certainly does when you come barging in right in the middle of our dinner! If you insist on airing this matter in public, at least be civilized about it!"

"Mr. Dikes," Michael said over the board president's choked-off rage, "what I'm doing is enforcing the rules adopted by your own board. Lonny is guilty of defacing school property, disobeying a teacher's direct order, and maintaining a generally disrespectful attitude toward that teacher. Any one of these alone adds up to a one-day suspension. I could have made it longer."

"Ha!" Dikes snorted. "Why not? Make a federal case out of a boy's minor infractions. And just what proof do you have of any of them? Besides *her*"—he glared at me—"word?"

Michael's voice crackled dangerously. "Is your son a liar?"

"What? By—"

"Because he confessed to defacing Ms. Carle's instructional material—"

"After you pressured him! Anybody could have stuck words on that disgraceful picture that shouldn't have been in the classroom, anyway."

"It did seem to pressure him, all right," Michael ground out, "when I confronted him with the magazine he'd stuffed behind his locker—the one he'd cut the letters from. It had *your* mailing label on it."

Dikes's mouth opened, then shut. "All right," he spluttered after a second's thought, "so the boy got a little feisty. There's no reason he has to serve the suspension tomorrow. It could just as well be Monday. And if he's having a problem with Ms. Carle, the answer is to get him out of her class and into something useful."

"The answer," Michael said, dangerously quiet, "is to apply the rules fairly to all students. And the rules say suspensions are served immediately. And after the first three weeks of a semester, classes may not be dropped for other than health reasons."

I thought Dikes was going to have a stroke. He swelled visibly with righteous indignation. "We'll see about this! I'll bring this before the whole board. If they'd listened to me in the first place, they wouldn't have added art to the curriculum. And I must have been nuts to let Ralph Jenks talk me into hiring a principal with *your* background. You're not running a big-city reform school here—"

"Harley Dikes, that's enough!" Miss Kellor's stern voice slammed him into momentary silence.

But, true to his nature, he resumed the attack. "All right, all right. I'll skip that. But I'll tell you, somebody was asleep at the wheel when they let my boy sign up for a class about as useful to him as a fur coat in July!"

"Dikes," Michael broke in, his patience at an end, "you keep referring to Lonny as your 'boy.' How long do you want him to be a boy? *He* chose his classes; *he* chose his behavior. Now let him accept the consequences. Like a man."

"Hmpf! He wouldn't be the first man to get lured into a stupid situation by a pretty face—"

Shadows and Secrets   47

Unimportant. Not useful. Stupid. Up to now I'd kept silent, but I'd heard myself and my chosen field belittled one too many times. "Mr. Dikes," I cut in icily, "art is not stupid." I stepped closer to the agitated man. "I don't know why Lonny signed up for my class, but I do know that if he wants to get something valuable out of it, he will."

"But he's no artist. He's a football player."

"So? Does that mean he's just a—a—bunch of cells? A robot running around with a football in his hands? Doesn't he have thoughts? Questions? Longings for something more than just what he can see and touch?"

Dikes's small, hard eyes left my intense ones; he fidgeted.

"You don't have to be a writer to get a spiritual lift from a book. But you do have to know how to read. I can help students 'read' art. They'll be the richer for it, even if it doesn't put a dime in their pockets."

"Well, I'm not going to argue with your highfalutin' theories. Maybe you've got a point. *But*—" Dikes refused to go down without trying one more ploy. "To get back to that suspension. . . . What about Coach Charles and the rest of the team? Is it fair to punish them by taking Lonny out of tomorrow night's game?"

Michael answered swiftly. "It's not fair that Lonny took himself out of the game by harassing an excellent teacher. But he did, the coach and the team know it, and Lonny would pay for it the rest of his life if they thought Lonny's 'daddy' got him off the hook.''

Dikes gritted his teeth. "All right; I'm not going to do anything to make things worse for my—for Lonny. But I give you fair warning. If I get word you're looking for chances to make life tough for the kid, Sauk Valley will be minus one art teacher and one principal. I guarantee it.''

Michael's lips formed a grim line. "Sir, I never have and never will make a disciplinary decision colored by fear of losing my job.''

Dikes glared at Michael, then Miss Kellor, finally me. It was hard to tell whether he was swearing vengeance under his breath or just trying to think of a blustering way out of an embarrassing situation. "So be it,'' he said gruffly. He turned and left.

Three deep breaths were drawn when Dikes's heavy-duty red pickup went thundering down the drive.

"I declare!'' Miss Kellor sighed. "I always knew Harley Dikes was bullheaded, but, of all people, he ought to understand the need for discipline. Why, he's a Vietnam veteran, decorated for carrying out orders under extreme hazard.''

"Well—'' Michael considered. "Dikes has lost his perspective when it comes to Lonny. But it *is* natural to go as far as you can to protect your own child. Isn't it?''

Miss Kellor started to disagree. Then her eyes caught

Shadows and Secrets 49

on Michael's; suddenly she turned off on, "Let's go in and finish our dinner, ruined though it may be. Actually, I think this calls for a good, stiff drink."

Miss Kellor repaired to the kitchen while Michael and I took our seats at the hastily deserted dining table.

"Michael," I began shyly, "did you mean what you said—about my being an excellent teacher?"

His eyes gentled, warmed. "You handle your job like a real pro, Mindi. I'm proud of you."

The praise poured around my heart like liquid gold. Not just because Michael's good opinion was so important to my career. But because of what I was learning *he* was. As a principal. As a man.

"But I'm still puzzled," I said. "About Lonny's attitude. I don't understand why he's taken such a dislike to me."

"Dislike?" Michael smiled into my eyes. "I don't think that's the problem. Before I let Lonny go today, we had a long talk. About how men get attention from women they feel attracted to. About how gentlemen don't try to bounce insults and smart talk off ladies they have a crush on."

"*What?* Are you saying Lonny has a crush on me?"

Michael nodded yes, still smiling.

"But—good night! I'm twenty-four! What do I have in common with a high-school boy?"

"That's just the trouble, my dear Ms. Carle. Lonny is no dummy; he realizes all that, and it's got him plenty frustrated. The kid's not so bad, but he's full of hormones and big ideas, Mindi. It's a tough time of life.''

"But there must be dozens of girls his age who'd be thrilled to go out with an Elvis Presley clone—"

Michael rose and came around behind my chair. He gently turned my head toward the mirror on the facing wall. "Take an objective look at yourself, portrait painter. There aren't dozens of girls of any age who've got what you've got."

I stared, fascinated. "What have I got?"

Michael's laughter feathered around my ear. "Don't you know what those big, soft eyes, that sweet, tender mouth do to a guy? Lonny Dikes has good taste; he just doesn't know what to do about it yet."

My heart did a crazy spin; I found myself trapped by the dark, powerful gaze holding mine in the mirror. I didn't realize Miss Kellor was back at the table until she set down a tray with three sparkling glasses.

"Here we are," she said, beaming. "Iced mint tea— with just a touch of bourbon."

Michael and I zapped back to the scene at hand. Spiked mint tea? Wow! Somehow we both managed not to laugh.

Chapter Five

Sauk Valley lost its Friday-night football game to arch rival Coal City by one point. Michael and I each took some heat from townspeople and students for keeping quarterback Lonny Dikes off the team. But, as Miss Kellor explained, most Sauk Valleyans expected quality education from their school system and realized it had to be well run and orderly to provide it. The fuss soon died down.

I didn't know what to expect when Lonny returned to class on Monday. At first he was quiet but sullen. But as the days went by and I maintained a firm, friendly attitude, he actually developed a reluctant interest in the class. Especially after I assigned Marietta

Page, the prettiest and most popular senior girl, as his partner for a research project.

Gradually my professional days were beginning to smooth out. It was a joy to discover how much raw artistic talent waited to be developed in the Sauk Valley schools. After the Lonny Dikes episode I was able to spend less energy corralling students' attention and focus more on that development.

Also, I could now relax a little and enjoy the social life of the Sauk Valley staff. Almost every weekend somebody put together a hot-dog roast, an after-game party, or some similar diversion. So when Lu Ann came up with the idea for a Halloween costume party in my loft studio, I was ready to listen.

"Can't you just see this place decorated all cobwebby and mysterious and the moon pouring in through the skylight?" she enthused. In the classroom Lu Ann was all facts. Out of it, she had a strong leaning toward the romantic.

"Can't you just feel us all getting drenched if it's a rainy night?" I teased. "Those stains on the north-end ceiling aren't abstract art!"

"Think positive, Min. Where there's a will, there's a way!"

Lu Ann and I decided "Come As Your Secret Self" would be a fun theme for our party. We also came up with some "rain insurance" for the north end of the loft: Nathan Kellor's big safari tent. We'd turn the loft

Shadows and Secrets 53

into a desert isle. True, there wasn't a logical connection between secret selves and desert isles, but it would beat getting soaked should the weather prove uncooperative.

Lu Ann and I overlooked a small detail in setting the last Friday in October for our masquerade ball. That was the date report cards were handed out for the first nine weeks. Amidst a frenzy of term-project evaluations, tests, and grade calculations, we eked out a half hour here and a minute there to make our party preparations.

We'd invited the entire school staff—cooks, bus drivers, custodians, and faculty. That's how things were done in Sauk Valley. By nine P.M. Halloween, just about all the partyers were in my studio. Except for Lu Ann and Michael.

Lu Ann and I had managed by ourselves to string dozens of "stars"—tiny amber Christmas lights—from the rafters. We'd lugged a half-dozen huge potted palms from the Kellor House back porch to stand around the loft, wafting atmosphere. But when it came to setting up the tent, we had to call on Michael's expertise. While he and Lu Ann worked to the last minute preparing the refreshment table inside the tent, I'd dashed off to throw on my costume in time to greet the first guests.

Now I checked the hors d'oeuvres table, groaning with rich and outrageous offerings brought by the staff.

That was another Sauk Valley custom. You never came to a party empty-handed.

Our guests had really gotten into the spirit of the affair. On the dance floor, Mr. Whitaker, a massive Julius Caesar in king-sized purple bed sheets, rocked out of sync with Mary, Queen of Scots, otherwise known as Miss Marie Kellor. Zeta Simms and her equally skinny husband, Fred, gyrated by as Arnold Schwarzenegger and Dolly Parton, hilarious in well-padded exercise suits.

Floyd Benson, head school custodian, had volunteered his deejay services for the night. He kept flinging back his shoulder-length hair and peering into his extensive disc collection through small wire-rimmed glasses. A leftover from the Flower Child era, Floyd was the only one of us who was perennially in costume.

I hummed to a late-sixties rock number. I loved to entertain. I loved to dance. I was all set to have a great time at my own party. Well—co-party.

"Terrific party!" Zeta declared, stopping for a nibble from the refreshment table. "And that's a great costume!"

"I didn't have time to get elaborate," I explained. I was a Left Bank artist in turtleneck sweater, slim skirt with a mid-thigh slit, silky hose, and high heels. All in black.

"If I had your body and gorgeous long legs, I'd

Shadows and Secrets   55

never wear anything else,'' Zeta swore. "And the red beret and scarf—perfect!"

Actually, my first plan had been to come as Toulouse-Lautrec in trousers bagged to my knees. However, this afternoon while we were setting up the tent, I'd noticed Michael giving Lu Ann a favorable once-over as she bent and stretched in her snug blue stirrup pants. In college it had never bothered me that Lu Ann attracted more men than I did. My hectic schedule didn't allow for much dating, anyway. But today, somehow it was different. Today I wondered if maybe Michael shouldn't notice there was more to *me* than just "big, soft eyes and sweet, tender mouth."

During a pause while Floyd Benson positioned a requested rap disc, a loud, brash "Yo ho ho, and a bottle o' *Bud*!" burst from the loft staircase. A shadow—a pirate's shadow—was cast ahead of someone ascending from the well-lighted garage below.

"Ahoy, mateys!" Black pants, boots, white shirt open to the waist, one gold earring, and an eye patch—Michael J. McCain stepped into the room, his wide grin almost smothered by a phony black beard. Everybody—including me—laughed and applauded when he did a few fast, accurate steps to the intense rap beat. My heart also did a fast, pleasurable turn as he made his way through the crowd to the hors d'oeuvres table.

"Sorry to be late," he said at my side. "But I just had a phone call from the local realtor. Guess what?

You won't have Old Blackbeard peering over your shoulder at Kellor House anymore."

"I won't?" Why did my heart take a sudden dive?

"The apartment below Lu Ann's. It's for rent as of next week."

"Oh?" Two months ago that news would have been music to my ears. But now— I covered my embarrassingly unenthusiastic reply with, "Here, have an hors d'oeuvre. I know you didn't have time for dinner."

"Glad to!"

One of the things I liked about Michael was his uninhibited enjoyment of good food. He searched over the loaded table and chose one of Lu Ann's specialties, cheese puffs filled with salmon pâté.

"Great stuff!" he pronounced, munching happily. Next his hand wavered between trays of Zeta's tangy sausage bits and my marinated beef strips; suddenly it dived into the basket of Lu Ann's Brie-stuffed mushrooms. As he bit into a luscious tidbit, his eyes widened in what I thought was pleasure with the hors d'oeuvre.

"Sen-*saa*-tional!" he mumbled through his fake whiskers.

That's when I noticed he was staring over my shoulder. Whistles and applause erupted behind me. I turned to see Lu Ann making her appearance. She'd said she'd probably have to wear her old Bozo the Clown outfit, since she, like me, had put so much time into the party

Shadows and Secrets 57

preparations. Right now I could have bopped her over her sleek blond head! Bozo the Clown, my foot!

As Marilyn Monroe, Lu Ann undulated to the center of the room, white halter dress, seductive facial mole, spiked white slides and all. I was upstaged, but good!

"H'lo, everybody. I hope," she whispered with a true Monroe lip quiver, "I hope I haven't come too late for the party."

Plenty of partyers, mostly male, hooted their assurance she could never be too late.

Jealousy wasn't a big part of my nature. But as I saw Michael's open appreciation of "Marilyn"—as well as her mushrooms—I smoldered! And he was going to live in the same apartment house with her?

It was a good thing Mr. Whitaker chose that moment to whirl me onto the dance floor in something of a cross between a polka and a cha-cha. Following my jovial Caesar's fancy footwork and small talk left me no time for brooding.

When I finally escaped Mr. Whitaker's clutches, I suffered a renewed attack by the green-eyed monster. Lu Ann was still garnering praise and laughter with her funny impersonation of the Magnificent Monroe. However, after she'd basked a while in the limelight, she pitched in and helped me keep everything rolling; I couldn't stay mad at her. Sure, it bothered me when Michael asked her to dance, but I had to admit there was nothing remotely steamy in their lighthearted capering around the floor.

It was getting close to midnight. I was wondering why Michael had danced with almost every female there except me. Sometimes when we'd pass each other on the floor, our eyes would meet, and a strange, fluttery sensation would stir my midriff. Something in his glance—a growing awareness—made me want his arms around *me*, his breath mingling with *mine*.

Then Floyd Benson tapped on an empty wine bottle to get everyone's attention. He'd already played "La Vie en Rose" in my honor. Now, he announced—a tad sloshily—that "for our other hip-chick hostess" he was going to play the theme song from Monroe's picture *Niagara*.

As the slow, throbbing strains of "Kiss" sifted from the stereo, I busied myself checking the tent refreshment table. I didn't want to get caught again by Mr. Whitaker. And I definitely didn't want to see Michael take some other lucky woman—like Lu Ann—into his arms for this dance.

I felt a strong, warm hand on my shoulder; my breath stopped as I hoped against hope.

"Would the most kissable woman in this room share a dance with a rowdy pirate?"

I turned around; the color rose in my face as I looked into Michael's uncovered eye, sparkling with teasing warmth. I hesitated a second; he took off his phony

Shadows and Secrets 59

beard and eye patch and cast them aside. Then we moved together into the most natural—and pleasurable—dance-embrace I'd ever known. Thanks to my high heels, my cheek was just right for nestling against Michael's. I drank in the enticing male aroma of clean skin and subtle after-shave. I followed the firm, close lead of his sinewy body as if I were second skin.

We turned, swayed, drifted to the compelling "Kiss." I knew this dance was special. Very, very special.

When the music ended, we found ourselves alone, between the back of the tent and the loft wall. We hadn't spoken once during the number, but now Michael's lips moved, just above mine.

" 'Kiss, kiss me—' " he repeated in a soft, caressing off-key.

I leaned against the back of the tent. I let my eyelids flutter seductively shut. *Please—be my guest! Kiss me!* I prayed as my heart pulsed in big, slow beats.

Michael's arms tightened around me with gentle power. "I've been hankering for this moment all evening, Ms. Beautiful Left-Bank Artist," he whispered, our lips a breath apart. "This old pirate's not much of a singer, but he *can* k—"

Thud! Someone inside the tent bumped against us so hard, we staggered comically into the opposite wall.

"Drat!" we heard in Mr. Whitaker's distinctive

rumble. "I knew this toga would trip me up before the night was out!"

For a couple of days following the Halloween party, Michael and I shared dozens of thrilling kisses—in my dreams. Actually, I tried to tell myself it was a good thing Mr. Whitaker had bumped me back into reality. Attractive as I found Michael, I had reservations about getting too close to him. There were too many unanswered questions.

What had sent him from Chicago South to the Minnesota woods? Not lack of administrative ability. Mr. Jenks was a hard act to follow, but Michael was rapidly winning over students and faculty alike with his unforced interest and calm competence in school affairs.

I kept remembering Miss Kellor's mysterious suggestion that Michael could trust Zeta with secrets. And Zeta's admission that he seemed to wear an airtight seal around his background.

Then there were those muffled-voice phone calls—the ones he took or made, often late at night, on the phone he'd had installed in Nathan's office. Business calls? Not likely.

Last but not least, there was that mean, dull scar on his lower back. It was too old to be caused by the car wreck, too uneven to be from surgery. What violence lay behind it?

All these things added up to a warning: Be careful!

Shadows and Secrets 61

Besides, if Michael felt anything really serious about me, would he be moving out of Kellor House within the week?

Then I found November was to be a month of surprises. First of all, Mr. Jenks, who was now recuperating from back surgery, decided to take early retirement. That meant Michael's term as principal would last the entire school year.

Second, the day before Michael was to move into his new apartment, he opted out. "I've been thinking it over," he told me at breakfast that morning. "I'm going to be busier than ever now. What little time I do have for household duties—well...."

He looked away; for once he seemed a little flustered. "I mean... Miss Kellor's been so nice to me, and she won't take another penny to pay for it. If I stayed on here, I could do some odd jobs. Like replacing all the shower heads. And chopping firewood from that fallen tree behind the carriage house. I'd like to help her out. That is... if *you* don't mind?"

My doubts about Michael weren't nearly as strong as my delight in having him under the same roof. I tried to remain casual as I assured him I didn't mind.

The third surprise wasn't so pleasant. My birthday was November ninth. All I received from my parents was a musty little card Mom must have gotten years ago in some box of all-occasion greetings. I don't know why I expected more. I'd suspected all my life I was an intruder into a marriage meant to be childless. It wasn't that Mom or Dad had looked for chances to be mean to me. But they had busy, carefully planned lives. It had always seemed easy for them to forget me—sort of out of sight, out of mind.

Surely, though, after twenty-five years, a little hint on my part might jog them into inviting me home for a birthday dinner. Or at least a cake. So on Saturday the eighth, I called them.

It would have been funny if it hadn't hurt so much, the polite surprise in Mom's voice. As if I were some shirttail cousin she liked but thought of seldom. She was terribly busy, she explained, because she and Dad had decided to go to Florida for the winter before Thanksgiving instead of after Christmas as they usually did. Perhaps I could run down to Florida "for a couple of days" during Christmas vacation? Oh, and by the way, she hoped I had a nice birthday.

The tears wouldn't be stopped; I held them all the way out of the house and to the foot of the stairs to my loft studio. I could hear the *chunk* of an ax biting into the downed tree behind the building, and I wanted to reach privacy before I let go. But suddenly the dam burst and I collapsed on the bottom step, sobbing.

"Want to talk about it?" A tanned, still-callused hand tucked a clean tissue into my fist.

I hated to seem like such a baby, but who could resist a voice so soft yet manly? Or a face concerned

Shadows and Secrets 63

and tender and only a foot from mine? Michael was kneeling to be on a level with me.

I told him what was wrong, what had always been wrong. He said nothing for a few moments. Then he lifted my face to his kind gaze.

"Mindi, I don't understand how anyone could forget a child's love. All I can say is your parents are the big losers, depriving themselves of you."

"I guess they don't see me as much of a prize."

Michael's eyes flashed with the green fire of emotion. "Listen, if I had a daughter turn out just like you, I'd be happy as a king!"

Some of the hurt I'd been carrying for a lifetime fell away in that instant. I knew Michael well enough now to know he believed what he was saying. We talked a while longer; Michael's upbringing had been rough and tumble, yet he treasured the strong family relationships it had forged.

"Know what, birthday girl?" he said at last. "I'm going in to call that restaurant in Galesburg—the one Lu Ann says is so fine. And you, I, and Miss Kellor are going stepping tonight! Steak, champagne—the works!"

"Oh, Michael! You don't have to do that—" I started to protest.

"Of course I don't have to," he said, rising. "I *want* to. Furthermore, I want your birthday cake delivered by singing waiters. And a ten-piece kazoo marching band!"

My laughter mingled with the tears still stinging my eyes.

That night, for the first time in my life, I knew what it was to be pampered, cherished—to be the temporary princess of a "family." The dinner and champagne were wonderful. The singing waiters delivered a magnificent cake. No kazoos, thank goodness. Miss Kellor gave me a topaz ring she'd worn since girlhood.

And Michael. When I saw through the candlelight how happy it made him to make *me* happy, how could I doubt him?

Chapter Six

"Are you sure this is where we turn off? This is a *cornfield!*"

Michael's new Bronco lurched over a rutted lane snaking through dried cornstalks.

He laughed. "I'm following Miss Kellor's directions to the letter. See, there's the timber she mentioned up ahead."

We were on our way to inspect Nathan Kellor's hunting lodge on the Illinois River, thirty miles west of Sauk Valley. The Sauk Valley Sportsmen's Club, led by—who else?—Harley Dikes, wanted to buy the lodge and its fifty acres of timber from Miss Kellor. She'd asked Michael to look it over and advise her as to a suitable asking price.

At the base of an extremely steep, wooded hill, the lane ended. We stepped from the Bronco into the mellow Sunday sun.

"There it is," Michael said, pointing to the low, weathered lodge atop the hill. It melted convincingly into the sparse brown leaves of November.

We found a rock-strewn path and made our way up the hill. Up close, the lodge looked shabby to me.

"Don't lean on that rail," Michael advised me as we walked out onto the deck overhanging a sharp bluff. "It looks a little wobbly."

I moved closer to him, and together we admired the stunning view of trees, rocks, and shining river below.

"Who'd ever believe there was a scene like this behind an ordinary cornfield?" I mused.

"You can thank the great glaciers for that," Michael said. "They pushed this area around pretty good a few thousand years ago."

His hand rested on my shoulder as he pointed to a thick patch of reeds some yards from the shore.

"See those pilings in the middle of the reeds? That's where Nathan Kellor had his duck blind," he said and proceeded to fill me in on some of the intricacies of the duck-hunting game.

"Okay, run that past me again," I kidded when he'd finished. "You're out from the crack of dawn till noon, sitting atop a narrow platform over forty-degree water, weeds higher than your head. Then you guys and the

Shadows and Secrets 67

wet retriever dogs go into the broken-down lodge to play cards and drink beer until it's time to fry a greasy dinner and go to bed early so you can get out at dawn the next day to do the same thing? All so you can shoot a bunch of poor little ducks?"

Michael grinned in answer to my needling. "Hey, your verbal portrait needs a couple of corrections. One: The dogs don't get in on the cards or beer—can't seem to handle either one. And two: You can't shoot 'a bunch of poor little ducks.' The state sets very tight limits on how many of what kind of ducks you can shoot. As a matter of fact, I'm not sure ducks don't have better protection than humans."

My eyebrow cocked doubtingly.

Michael gave my shoulder a playful cuff. "You don't understand hunting and men, Mindi. It may not be the noblest thing we do, but it gives us a chance to get uncivilized for a while. Without doing too much damage."

"But do the *ducks* see it that way?"

"Come on, Conscience," he said with an amused shrug. "Let's check out the lodge."

Inside we found one large all-purpose room and four bedrooms, all musty smelling and in need of a good scrub. A wood-burning stove served for cooking and heating, kerosene lanterns provided light, and water came by way of an outdoor pump. The "bathroom" was an old-fashioned outhouse situated some thirty yards from the lodge.

We took a leisurely ramble through the woods crowning the hill, then down through a ravine and out across a brief meadow to the edge of another wooded patch. Suddenly Michael's hand clasped my forearm, stopping me in my tracks.

"Look," he whispered, "over there, by that big oak tree."

It took me a second to see the tall, graceful buck whitetail; then a shaft of light played over its antlers as the deer turned and melted into the woods, silent and elusive as a shadow.

Michael's grip had slid down my jacket sleeve to my hand. He didn't say anything, but I could tell by his half smile and the softness in his eyes he was as moved by the buck's beauty as I was.

The thought burst from me on impulse. "It's hard for me to understand, Michael."

He glanced down at me, questioning. "Understand what?"

"Well—you, up in Minnesota—killing for sport. You don't seem the type."

His black brows pulled together. "I didn't kill for sport. I was a guide. It was my job."

"Okay. But you helped others track and kill animals."

"I had obligations, Mindi, that had to be met. And

Shadows and Secrets

for that time in my life, that was the best way I could meet them."

I wanted to ask him *why,* but I resumed walking, silent.

"If it'll make you feel better, the only times I fired a gun were when I had to track down some wounded animal and finish it off."

I stopped. "Didn't that bother you? The slaughter of innocent animals?"

He took both my arms and turned me to look into his determined gaze. "Look, I don't get any kick out of taking life, not even an animal's. But I'm not a vegetarian. And I never guided a hunting party that wasn't going to dress out its kills and use them for food. And I'll tell you right now—" His voice gathered vehemence. "I worry a lot more about the slaughter of innocent human beings than the controlled killing of anything on four feet." He dropped my arms and stepped back. "I'm sorry if that offends you, Mindi, but. . . ." He left the rest of the sentence unsaid.

I sighed. "Chalk one up for you, Michael. I just remembered how good that steak tasted last night. And how much I love this new leather jacket I'm wearing. Peace?"

He grabbed my hand again, smiling companionably. "Peace!"

We headed back toward the lodge.

"So, do you think Miss Kellor could get much for

this property?" I asked when we'd stepped back inside the lodge again.

"With a riverfront for fishing as well as duck shoots, plus cornfields behind it to attract pheasant and deer? It's an Illinois hunter's dream! Miss Kellor can expect a good price from the Sauk Valley Sportsmen's Club."

"With Harley Dikes the head of it?" I scoffed. "He probably thinks he'll get it by force of personality! *Poison* personality, that is."

"We'll find out. The club is coming over to rebuild the duck blind and do some shooting next weekend. They've invited me to come along as Miss Kellor's representative."

"Michael," I groaned, incredulous, "you're going to be cooped up all weekend with that squinty-eyed, fat-faced Harley Dikes? The mere thought chills me!"

Michael was examining the lantern hung above the kitchen table. "He's a bullhead and a big mouth, but I've known worse men."

"Ugh!"

Michael turned toward me slowly; a shadow played momentarily across his features. "Mindi, you say you're fascinated by faces. Have you ever looked straight into the face of evil?"

I was taken aback; finally I shook my head. "No—I don't think so."

"If you had, you'd know, honey. And you'd know why I don't worry too much about Harley Dikes."

Shadows and Secrets

His somber mood lasted only seconds, but even after he jokingly challenged me to a race back to the Bronco, I was haunted by the darkness of that moment. Something—someone—had done Michael J. McCain terrible harm.

We ate dinner that night at the Duck Inn, a funny little place ten miles from the lodge. The inn—which included a bowling alley—branched out willy-nilly from a main dining room about the size of a postage stamp.

Serenaded through the wall by the ever-present *thwok* of bowling balls careening down alleys and into pins, we ate biscuits and Burgoo Stew. The menu said the pioneer delicacy was, by tradition, made from whatever game and vegetables were available. I had no idea what was in it but, shared with Michael, it was heavenly.

Thanksgiving was the first holiday in years when I hadn't felt more or less at loose ends. Miss Kellor, assured by Michael and me that we'd fare well on our own, accepted an invitation to spend the day with a friend across town. I looked forward to producing my first holiday feast. I intended to show off a bit for Michael.

The popcorn fight started Thanksgiving afternoon as I took two plump "victims" of the Great Duck Shootout from the freezer.

"You ever cooked wild duck before?" Michael wanted to know.

"No. But as you say, hunting spoils shouldn't be wasted. Besides, the recipe looks easy." I washed my hands and dumped some freshly made popcorn into a bowl.

"Duck's not the easiest game to prepare, you know," Michael said, dipping into the popcorn. "Now, if you want my advi—"

"Sorry. One cook to the broth," I announced airily.

Miss Kellor was the acknowledged top chef at Kellor House, but Michael and I were locked in lively competition for second place.

"You don't like my cooking?" he accused, tossing a corn kernel into the air and catching it on his tongue.

I grinned. "Let's just say you lean pretty heavily on the can opener. And you don't know beans about fat, cholesterol, or sugars." I bent to look in a lower cupboard for a roasting pan.

"Don't wanta know about 'em, either." Pling! A corn kernel flicked off my rear jeans pocket.

That started the war. I grabbed a handful of popcorn and whipped it toward Michael. The first thing we knew, we were both slinging popcorn, giggling and dodging and running all over the house. Michael caught me in the center hall and tried to cram a handful of corn down the back of my sweater. I escaped and bounded up the spiral staircase with him right behind

Shadows and Secrets

me. I tore down the upstairs hallway and down the back staircase. Just as I reached the bottom, he caught me. We struggled over who was going to do what with popcorn; then my foot slipped off the bottom step. Suddenly we found ourselves lying side by side on the stairs.

We were both laughing so hard, we were breathless. When he could, Michael raised up on one elbow and ran a hand through the black hair spilling all over his forehead. He was looking down at me, his grin gradually changing to a slow, tender smile.

"You've got the cutest grin," he said huskily. "You make me feel good all over when you smile."

"Even though I've got a—a space between my front teeth?" I asked, all at once shy.

"Especially because you've got that space between your teeth!" he vowed. His voice lowered to a whisper, and his free hand touched my face. "I *love* that space between your teeth!"

The kiss I'd been longing for ever since Halloween followed, as natural as breath. It was worth the wait. His lips started as gentle velvet on mine. And then he kissed me again. And once more. Each time his arms pulled me closer, his lips stirred me deeper.

"I—I think I'd better take care of those ducks," I finally squeaked.

"Yeah," he murmured, his mouth still dangerously

warm near mine. He sat up, unwillingly, I thought.
"Yeah, and I'd better clean up the popcorn."

I rose and opened the door to the kitchen. Michael stopped me with a hand on my arm. "Mindi, I just want you to know—it's been a long time since I've laughed so much, had such a fun time. You—you're good for me."

I stepped down into the kitchen and began to do things toward dinner. But my mind worked in a silky haze. It shouldn't matter so much to me, what Michael had just said. But it did. Oh, it did!

Dreamily I headed down the hall to the drawing room to set us an elegant table before the great marble fireplace. What was that by the staircase?

I picked up a wallet—Michael's. It must have slipped out of his back pocket while we were roughhousing. Something had fallen from it—a picture of a little girl.

I took one look, and I was stunned. Bone structure, skin coloring, green eyes, black hair—everything but the dainty little nose. That child was Michael's!

"Mindi—"

Michael had come up behind me. I had the strangest feeling when I looked into his face. I trusted him; I liked him so very much. But of all the shadows around his background, this one shook me most.

"That's—my niece. Erin," he said.

Shadows and Secrets 75

For the first time since I'd met him, I didn't believe him.

"She—uh—she lives near Chicago. She's—my sister's child," he added lamely.

"She's beautiful, Michael. It's very apparent you're—related."

He took the picture from me, avoiding my eyes. "Yeah. I think the world of her."

That was all that was said about Erin, but her sparkly gaze and happy smile burned in my memory. I knew as surely as I stood there that she was Michael's child. Why he was lying about that fact?

I went back to the kitchen, mulling the situation. But I wanted so much for this to be a Thanksgiving feast to be remembered. Deliberately, I shook off my questions and plunged into food preparation. I wanted to have plenty of time for a warm, luxurious bath and a long, careful session before my makeup mirror.

The wild rice with tiny onions was simmered; the fresh fruit in honey dressing was tastefully arranged on salad plates; the orange sauce sat hot and piquant, waiting to be lavished over the duck.

Ah! Now for the pièce de résistance! Slowly I opened the oven door; carefully I removed the baking pan and sniffed the tantalizing aroma of roast duck. Reverently, I approached the nicely browned fowl with the testing fork.

Spr-o-o-n-g! The fork bounced off Duck Number One like a rocket! What— I tried again, this time with Duck Number Two. Same results!

I grabbed Miss Kellor's old-time *Wild Fowl Cookbook*. Two glasses of champagne had made me a little woozy, but I found the recipe for duck a l'orange. *Bake in hot oven 35–40 min.*

"Hmm. What does 'hot' mean? Maybe if I turn up the thermostat and give them another ten minutes—"

I turned up the heat and set the oven timer. I smoothed the skirt of the rosy-red velvet sheath dress I'd been saving for a special occasion and went back to the drawing room.

Michael stood with his back to a roaring fire, absolutely devastating, to my way of thinking, in a beautifully tailored dark suit. He saluted me with an appreciative grin and a hoisted champagne glass.

"Sure I can't help you in the kitchen, Mindi?"

"Everything's under control," I assured him with a confidence I didn't feel.

We nibbled a few more hot canapés—*they'd* turned out well, thank goodness!—and shared some long, warm glances over the rims of our glasses. Then I heard the faint ding of the oven timer and excused myself to the kitchen.

I held my breath as I tried to spear Duck Number One. Still tough as a rock!

"Ducks," I muttered, "I've given you every

Shadows and Secrets

chance. Now, you stubborn little twerps jolly well better get tender, and fast!'' I gave the oven regulator a savage twist as far to the left as it would go.

Back in the drawing room, I tried to concentrate on small talk and at the same time wonder what I was going to do if the ducks didn't take a turn for the better. After ten minutes of agony I decided it was now or never for the stars of my Thanksgiving show. I headed for the kitchen, Michael following me.

Heat and smoky fumes met us at the door.

I grabbed the cooking mitts and flung open the oven. The ducks looked like dreams! Dark, golden brown, sizzling in their own juices. Triumphantly I prepared to lift them onto a platter and bathe them in orange sauce.

"Let me help," Michael insisted. He took the two cooking forks to lift Duck Number One—or was it Two? No matter. He stabbed; the forks actually clattered as they hit the now-baked-to-ceramic skins!

My gorgeous dinner! Ruined!

My face was already red from the oven heat, but now it blazed like a peony as Michael turned to me with a what-did-I-tell-you? grin.

"You did something to these birds, didn't you, to make them uncookable!" I accused angrily.

He broke into open laughter. "I've never touched those ducks. I didn't even shoot 'em."

"But—you brought them back. I mean—I thought—" I sputtered to a halt.

Michael could hardly speak for the laughter doubling him. "Harley Dikes—those are Dikes's ducks!" he gasped helplessly.

"What kind of trick is this? I don't think it's funny!"

"It's no trick, Mindi," Michael said, wiping his eyes. "After you gave me that bad time about hunting, I didn't even take my gun to the lodge. Because I've never yet eaten a wild duck that was worth the killing of it. Dikes, being a crack shot, naturally, got his limit the first day. He insisted on sending a couple to Miss Kellor."

"Dikes's ducks—I wasted all that time and effort trying to make something special out of Dikes's ducks?"

Suddenly the ridiculousness of the situation hit me. I began to laugh, and the more I chortled, the more Michael guffawed. We ended up clinging to each other, howling in uncontrollable glee.

When Miss Kellor came home at ten, she found Michael and me in front of the drawing-room fireplace, all dressed up and dining in style. On wild rice with tiny onions, and fresh fruit in honey dressing. And—hot dogs a l'orange!

Chapter Seven

"**D**on't look now, Mindi," Lu Ann muttered out of the corner of her mouth, "but I think there's a man following you."

It was the Saturday after Thanksgiving. Lu Ann, Zeta, and I were treating ourselves to the official opening of the Christmas shopping season in Chicago. Right now Lu Ann and I were on an up escalator at the pricey Water Tower Place mall.

"What's he look like? And in this mob, how can you tell he's following me?" I asked. The Tower was packed with eager shoppers.

"He's definitely noticeable. Tall, blond, and yum-*yum*," Lu Ann murmured from her sideways vantage point. "He's been staring at your back, and now"—

she pivoted smoothly to step off the escalator—"he's walking up right behind you!"

I hopped off the escalator and turned to see who was behind me.

"Why—Brett? Brett Campbell!"

The big, good-looking man in a black leather bombadier's jacket broke into a wide grin.

"Mindi! I've been trying to catch up with you the past five minutes! How's it goin', kid?"

Brett was a few years older than I, and a journalist. He'd just landed a job with the *Chicago Tribune* when we met at the Kane vs. Kane divorce trial. There was nothing between us but friendship. He'd admired my illustrative skills, and I'd admired his uncanny ability to ferret out facts and weave them into a riveting story.

I introduced him to Lu Ann; then he and I began a quick exchange of news. But we were holding up traffic.

Brett looked at his watch. "It's almost twelve. How about the three of us taking in some lunch?"

Lu Ann and I were supposed to meet Zeta at a mall restaurant within the hour. But I could see an interested gleam in Lu Ann's eye as she took in Brett's rugged physique and thick mop of dark-blond curls. I had a sudden inspiration. "I'd love to, Brett, but I've got another commitment at one."

Brett's reaction was exactly what I'd hoped it would be. "That's too bad, Mindi." He turned to Lu Ann

Shadows and Secrets

with a cajoling smile. "Maybe you could spare an old newshound a half hour over the best beer and brats in Chicago?"

"I could manage," she said lightly.

Lu Ann needed no more help from me. I sent her off on Brett's arm with my silent blessing.

Now I'd have a few minutes alone to ponder a decision I had to make.

In spite of steady income since September, my funds were running on low. I had a college loan to pay off and a professional wardrobe to acquire. I'd checked on round-trip airfare to Florida. It was clear: I could pay a duty call on my parents in Florida for a couple of days after Christmas. Or I could buy something meaningful for each of the people who were becoming dearer to me every day—Lu Ann, Zeta, Miss Kellor. And, of course, Michael. But I couldn't do both.

I stared through a shop window at a mannequin family cozily singing carols around a glorious tree. In the next window, mannequin children reveled in torn wrappings and delightful gifts while Mom and Dad glowed happily in the background.

Christmas had never been like that for me. Mom was always pushing to get the "mess" cleared up. After all, she had to cook dinner for the two or three relatives she couldn't avoid inviting. Dad was always in a foul mood because he was going to have to be nice to the relatives.

And the gifts. What a chore they were for Mom! She wore herself out trying to find bargains on "practical" items. Not that she was poor. She and Dad had both held down good jobs.

I used to wish that just once they'd let themselves go and give me one small, silly gift. Give it with their full, loving attention.

I sighed, debating whether or not to make one more attempt to pierce the high, smooth wall separating me from my parents' affections. I thought of Miss Kellor at home right now baking and freezing all kinds of delicacies for the big Christmas dinner she served to some two dozen "unattached" Sauk Valleyans every year.

I thought of Michael asking her last night if she'd mind a big, live evergreen dropping needles in the drawing room.

Mind? Oh, for an old-fashioned tree with tinsel and glitter!

And there were Zeta and Fred. Unable to have children, they collected and repaired items all year long for Toys for Tots.

I considered Lu Ann's cordial invitation to spend any or all of the school holiday with her and her family in Springfield.

My mind was made up. I walked into the nearest card shop and picked out a handsome holiday greeting. The card, accompanied by a box of good candy, would go to Florida. I would stay in Sauk Valley.

Shadows and Secrets 83

I felt as if I'd just thrown off a ten-ton burden. Now I could do what I'd always longed to do—buy beautiful gifts for people who'd love getting them as much as I'd love giving them.

By the time Lu Ann, Zeta, and I met at Lu Ann's car to return to Sauk Valley, two of us were exhausted. Zeta and I carried loaded shopping bags; Lu Ann bore nothing but a satisfied smile.

"Well, I can tell by the look on your face you had the best brats and beer in Chicago," I kidded her as she pulled out of the parking deck. "I take it you found Brett Campbell—likable?"

"He's okay," Lu Ann said. "I mean—great looks, fascinating job, and single—I can stand him."

"It figures," Zeta said with a wry wink at me. "I go shopping and get tired feet and a pair of overpriced red pajamas for Fred. Mobley goes to market and comes out with a man!"

Zeta began full-scale pumping for information about Lu Ann's afternoon. I'd have paid more attention to Lu Ann's droll description of the lunch, the tour of the *Tribune* Tower, and Brett's expressed interest in seeing her again, but I was ruminating happily over the gaily wrapped packages in my shopping bag.

For Lu Ann I'd found a pair of gold-trimmed blue enamel earrings. What they'd do for her already stunning face and eyes was practically criminal. Of course,

I had a hunch Brett Campbell might draw her off Michael's scent, so I could afford to be above jealousy.

Zeta and Fred were into antiquing. I'd gotten them a book Zeta had mentioned as a veritable antique identification bible.

For Miss Kellor it was a soft, pink wool cardigan sweater, imported from Ireland. The price was high. But she was so pretty in pink. And Kellor House was drafty in winter.

I'd had to pace back and forth in front of Michael's gift several times. Wasn't I a fool to pay so much for a fountain pen? A fountain pen was yuppie, and Michael wasn't. But it was so handsome. Marbled gray with eighteen-karat gold trim and nib. I kept seeing it wrapped in Michael's strong, sensitive fingers. I kept remembering Michael's kindnesses, Michael's kisses.

I'd bought it.

There was someone else I couldn't forget. Erin. I kept seeing her small, happy face. I wondered how many times a day Michael thought of her. How much did he miss her? Slowly, the idea for another gift for him, a private, very special one, began to take shape in my mind.

It would take some real planning. And espionage. I fell into a doze plotting it as Lu Ann's little red Beretta scooted down the 130 miles separating Chicago from Sauk Valley....

* * *

I felt like the world's biggest sneak. It was the Monday following the shopping spree at Water Tower Place. Six o'clock of a dark, snowy morning, to be exact. I slipped a furtive hand into the wallet lying on Brother Nathan's huge mahogany desk; I searched for what I needed, found it, and crept soundlessly out of the room and across the hall.

Once inside my own room, I let out my pent breath and propped the small photograph in my hand against an easel. I got my Polaroid and snapped a close-up. It seemed like hours instead of seconds before the picture slid out of the camera.

I checked it. Yes, it would do.

I held the original photo under a strong light and stared at it, absorbing every nuance of a spirited, intelligent little face. It would be doing it the hard way, painting a portrait from a photo and a photo of a photo. In a way, though, I had a live model. Except for the nose, I could see the child in the father. And I wouldn't mind studying him at all, I mused as I slunk hurriedly across the hall to return Erin McCain's picture to her sleeping daddy's wallet. . . .

Mr. Dikes was at it again. I'd been operating under the delusion that since Lonnel was doing pretty well in my class and since the semester course soon would be finished, Mr. Dikes was off my case. Wrong.

Michael came home late the next night from a

school-board meeting. Miss Kellor had gone to bed, and I was in the den watching *It's a Wonderful Life* for possibly the fortieth time.

"Mindi," Michael said, settling tiredly into an easy chair, "tell me about the Snowball royalty election today. You were in charge of the vote count, weren't you?"

"Well—yes," I said, mystified. Since I was the only teacher without a full-time club or class sponsorship, I'd been put in charge of the upcoming Snowball, Sauk Valley High's big holiday formal.

"Was there anything—irregular about it—the vote count, I mean?" Michael quizzed.

I snapped off Jimmy Stewart right in the middle of his drowning scene. "No. Marietta Page won in a breeze for Snow Queen. For the boys it was very close."

"And Lonny Dikes missed being the Snow King by two votes?"

I groaned. "Don't tell me—Mr. Dikes thinks there was something funny about the voting?"

Michael nodded, eyes closed. "You've got it. The world is going to hell in a hand basket—and Harley Dikes is all bent out of shape because his son is only *second* most popular boy in school!"

I jumped out of my chair. "Now, that makes me furious!" I stormed. "I recounted the ballots twice just to be sure—"

Shadows and Secrets

"Hold it, Mindi," Michael cautioned. "Who else was with you?"

"I took the ballots to Zeta's office. But she got called out before we'd finished counting. It never occurred to me anybody would think I'd cheat!"

Michael waved me down. "I don't doubt your honesty," he said. "But Dikes assumes the worst. He thinks you've got it in for Lonnel."

"That's rubbish, and you know it, Michael!"

"Of course I do. In the future, anytime you count votes, be sure to call in a student council member or another teacher. By the way, where are the Snowball ballots?"

My stomach twisted. "I was supposed to save them?"

Michael rubbed his forehead. "Somehow I knew you were going to say that. Look, it's my fault. I should have warned you to save them."

"That miserable Harley Dikes!" I fumed. "I suppose he brought this—this 'scandal' up before the whole board?"

"No. Not yet, at least. He cornered me before the meeting tonight to tell me *he* wants a look at the ballots too."

I was flabbergasted. "That is the most childish, small-minded, ridiculous—" I sputtered, out of breath.

"I quite agree. But Dikes was looking for trouble tonight. You see, Miss Kellor is balking now about selling

Brother Nathan's hunting facilities to the Sauk Valley Sportsmen's Club. Says she just can't bring herself to let go of them yet. Naturally Dikes thinks I've convinced her to hold out for some sky-high price."

"Oh, this is just great! I'm breaking my back to make this a beautiful dance! Staying after school every night to oversee the decorations some of my art students are designing and making. Up to my ears in band contracts and refreshments and lining up chaperones. And now I'm accused of vote tampering?"

"Mindi, honey, could you tone it down? I've already got a headache."

"Oh. Sorry! But Dikes makes me so mad," I muttered half under my breath.

Michael loosened his tie and laid his head on the chair back. He closed his eyes again and didn't say anything for a few seconds. Then a rueful grin spread slowly across his face.

"I don't think it's anything to laugh about," I snapped.

He chuckled wryly. "I was just thinking about some of the problems that come up in a big-city school. Believe me, Mr. Dikes qualifies as a minor annoyance."

I started an angry response, but I thought of Michael's two years in the North Woods, of the ugly red scar on his back. I bit back my words.

"Come on, Mindi, let's call it a day," Michael said,

wearily getting to his feet. "We'll get this tempest in a teapot settled tomorrow."

He switched off the lights, and the two of us wound our way up the spiral staircase, Michael still chuckling and I gnashing my teeth over the irascible Harley Dikes.

Of course, Mr. Dikes was at school first thing next morning. Michael had just called me in to meet with him, when Zeta came into the office.

"Excuse me, Ms. Carle; you left these ballots in my office yesterday," she said. "So I saved them." With her back to Mr. Dikes she glanced significantly at the waste can.

I managed not to sigh with relief.

I held my breath while Michael and Harley Dikes counted 147 ballots—the exact number of students present at Sauk Valley High yesterday when the vote was taken.

"All right," Mr. Dikes said grumpily as the last vote was tallied. "Joe Jensen still comes out two votes ahead. But what about the absentee ballots?"

"What absentee ballots?" I queried.

"Surely you're going to let the five students who weren't here yesterday vote?" Dikes barked. "This is an all-school affair, isn't it?"

The line of healed stitches on Michael's forehead began to show, the way they did when he got tense. "There's nothing in the school guidelines about absentee voting."

"Is there anything *against* it?" Dikes demanded.

Michael's lips pulled together. I could tell Mr. "Minor Annoyance" was getting to him. He walked around behind his desk. "Ms. Carle," he said with forced calm, "you're the dance sponsor. Would you object to letting the absentees vote?"

"But I've already announced the winners!" I protested.

"And you shouldn't have, should you, Ms. Carle?" Dikes charged. "You should have checked with someone experienced in these things before you made any announcements."

The fact that Dikes was half right made me all the more furious. But what could I say? "If it means that much to you, Mr. Dikes, let the absentees vote."

"Fine!" he boomed. "I just want Lonny to get a fair shake."

While I turned inside out with anger at Mr. Dikes and chagrin at my own lack of foresight, Michael called in the five students absent yesterday and handed them ballots.

Then I counted their votes, Dikes breathing right down my neck. The first one was for Joe; the next three for Lonny. My hand started to tremble as I unfolded vote five. My stomach plummeted right into my shoes. It was for Lonny.

"Well!" Dikes crowed. "I guess that puts the matter right, doesn't it? Won by one vote!"

Shadows and Secrets 91

I could feel hot tears forming behind my eyelids, but I took a deep breath and squared my shoulders. "I'll tell Joe," I said. "And Lonny." I started for the door.

"Wait." Michael came around the desk. "Before you do that, I think we should call Lonny in."

Dikes looked puzzled. "What for? He's won the election fair and square."

"But it's his friend, Joe Jensen, who's going around thinking he's king. Let's let Lonny know what's happened before we say anything to Joe."

Mr. Dikes grumbled, but Michael called in Lonny, anyway. He came to the office looking a little nervous in spite of his cocky Elvis pompadour.

It took all my resolution, but I choked out an explanation of why he was there.

"You're the king, now, son," Mr. Dikes said proudly. "I knew you'd be up there with Marietta when we got this straightened out."

Lonny's face reddened. "Dad, I asked you not to do this—"

"But you *won*," Dikes Senior insisted. "Fair and square."

Lonny's sturdy young throat bobbled in a hard swallow. "I don't want to be king. I mean, not that way. Joe's real set up about winning, and the *Weekly Shopper* has taken pictures of him and Marietta. I—I just wouldn't feel right about takin' it away from him."

Mr. Dikes started spluttering. "Is this school making

a sissy out of you? When you win fair and square, you don't throw it away!"

Lonny's throat bobbled again. Plainly it cost him to stand up to his father. "No, Dad."

There was nothing for Dikes to do but back off. Michael courteously escorted him to the door, and he went off, muttering.

"I'm sorry if I bumbled the election, Lonny," I said. "Thank you for being so big about it." I held out my hand. Shyly Lonny's big paw accepted it.

"That's okay, Ms. Carle," he murmured, flushing to the roots of his golden hair. "It kind of makes up for—well—you know."

After he'd gone, I sank onto a chair. "Thank goodness Zeta got those ballots out of her wastebasket! And thank goodness you were right about Lonny Dikes being a good kid. But do you still maintain Harley Dikes is just a minor pain in the neck?"

"Yup. I do."

Sometimes Michael's convictions were just plain stubborn.

The Snowball went off without any more major hitches. Naturally, one carload of boys came beered up. Michael met them at the door with a calm reminder they'd be on suspension as of Monday. Then he called their parents to come get them.

Otherwise the night seemed to be a grand success. I had to smile at the magic wrought by fancy dresses and rented tuxedos. Daytime rowdies turned into nighttime ladies and gentlemen.

Lonnel Dikes, resplendent in white tails, applauded heartily when Marietta and Joe led the first dance as King and Queen of the Snowball. Then he chose as his partner the quiet little wallflower serving punch. I watched her pale face light up. If an election were held tomorrow, Lonny Dikes would get her vote. For anything.

Chapter Eight

"**I**n the middle of a project?"

Lu Ann moved from the doorway into my bedroom.

"Almost finished," I answered, deftly covering the small canvas on the easel in my big window alcove. December was no month to work in my loft studio.

"Hmm. Secret project, is it?" Lu Ann asked, grinning.

"I never show a work in progress. Don't want anybody to see my mistakes." I smiled and invited Lu Ann to share a pot of tea with me downstairs.

While the tea steeped and I got out some of my fabulous caramel-topped double-fudge brownies—made with skim milk—Lu Ann and I indulged in casual chit-chat. I had a feeling, though, she had something on her mind she'd bring up when the time was right.

"Have you, uh, settled on your holiday plans yet, Mindi?" Lu Ann asked, preparatory to biting into a brownie.

"Mmm-hm. I'm going to stay here, help Miss Kellor with her big Christmas dinner."

"Oh? And how about Michael? I suppose he's going to stick around to carve the turkey?"

I tried to answer nonchalantly. "I have no idea what his plans are. Why?"

"Just want to make sure I've lost out to you before *I* pursue other options, Min— Ummmh! These brownies are *scrumptious!*"

"Lost out to *me?*" I feigned total innocence.

Lu Ann grinned and licked a bit of caramel from her lower lip. "Don't play coy with me, toots. I saw you and Michael dance around behind the tent at our Halloween Ball. And all of a sudden his move to the apartment below mine was off."

"Lu Ann, Michael only stayed on here to fix up some things for Miss Kellor. Why, he's put in new shower heads, cleaned up an old tree, replaced a window in the cupola—"

"You're babbling, honey," Lu Ann said amusedly. "Well, you can't fool me. I've seen that old 'Isn't she lovely?' light in his eyes when he thinks no one's looking—"

Shadows and Secrets

"Stop it, Lu Ann," I commanded. "You're imagining things. We're just friends. Good friends."

"Sure. Sure," Lu Ann agreed with a sage nod. "*Good* friends. Well, don't apologize." She laughed, a teasing sparkle in her wide blue eyes. "Because it seems I'm developing a new friendship too."

"Aha! Let me guess—are his initials B.C.?"

"Bingo!"

"That's great, Lu Ann!" My heart did a little dance to know a potential rival was off the chase—and happily so. "So tell me what's going on."

Lu Ann filled me in on the phone calls between her and Brett Campbell since I'd introduced them two weeks ago. She'd kept quiet about them till now, waiting for him to suggest something solid in the way of a get-together.

"Some of the high mucky-mucks at the *Tribune* are throwing a big Christmas party December twenty-second," she explained. "Brett's asked me to be his date."

"That's the day school vacation starts. You're going, aren't you?" I urged.

Lu Ann inspected her long, bright-pink nails. "As a matter of fact, I do think I've got time in my busy social calendar for champagne, caviar—and a few hours with one handsome dude!"

We launched into a long, intense discussion of clothes, hairstyles, and mental attitudes suitable for big-city social fetes. Lu Ann finally rose from the kitchen table to take her leave. She paused in the zipping of her jacket.

"Min—" she said hesitantly, "if this weekend goes okay— Well, remember Zeta talking about having a New Year's Eve party?"

"Yes?"

"Well, I may invite Brett down for it. That is, if I can find him somewhere to stay."

I wasn't sure what Lu Ann was getting at. "There's the motel—"

"Mindi, it's—a little rustic, if you know what I mean. What I was wondering is—you don't suppose Miss Kellor could put him up for a couple of nights, do you? For pay, of course," she added quickly.

"I don't know," I said. "I guess you could ask her."

"Actually, since Brett's your friend, too, I was wondering if *you* would ask her."

I had some doubts about Miss Kellor's reaction. She wasn't running a bed-and-breakfast. I'd hate for her to think I was presuming upon her hospitality.

Yet I hated to douse the hopeful gleam on Lu Ann's horizon. Out here in Sauk Valley, how often would she cross paths with a Brett Campbell?

"Okay," I agreed. "I'll check into it, Lu."

Lu Ann dashed to my side for a quick hug. "Thanks, Min! I just know this is going to be a great New Year's Eve!"

Shadows and Secrets 99

"I hope so. I've been through so many that were clown-city. You know, everybody trying too hard to have the best night of the year."

Lu Ann gave my shoulders another squeeze. "Don't I know! But this year will be different. And not just because I've got a dream date. Zeta and Fred know how to throw a really fun party. You and Michael *are* going to be there, aren't you?"

"I am. But I don't know what Michael's plans are."

"He's counting on spending New Year's Eve with you, Min; I'd bank on it!"

After Lu Ann left, I allowed myself a few seconds of daydreaming. If others could see it, maybe Michael felt at least half as much interest in me as I felt in him?

Later on, in my room, I took the cover from the small canvas on the easel. I'd fibbed to Lu Ann. Actually, the four- by six-inch oil portrait was finished.

I gazed at the child's face, the dark hair and great emerald eyes that had haunted me since the day I first saw them. Her mouth—the hardest part of any portrait—I believed I'd gotten that just right.

The portrait was good. Now all I needed was the appropriate moment to give it to Michael.

The last week of school before vacation was also the end of the first semester. In the flurry of tests and grade figuring, I didn't get around to asking Miss Kellor about renting a room to Brett Campbell.

"I'll do it tonight," I promised Lu Ann on December 21. Yet when I got home to Kellor House after school, I still waffled over the matter. Somehow I sensed it wasn't going to go over too well with Miss Kellor.

But as we did the dinner dishes, I summoned my nerve. "Miss Kellor, the Simmses are planning a New Year's Eve party."

"Yes, I know," Miss Kellor said, swishing rinse water over a soapy plate. "They've invited me to come, which I think is very sweet of them."

"Yes, well, uh—Lu Ann's bringing a friend from Chicago—actually, he's *my* friend, too."

"Really?" Miss Kellor turned interested eyes on me. "What a lucky young man!"

"Yes, well, uh—he's a fascinating person. You may have seen his bylined articles in the *Chicago Tribune*. Brett Campbell?"

The faintest shade of reserve darkened Miss Kellor's clear blue eyes. "Oh—a newsman?"

"Yes. And Lu Ann is a little apprehensive about putting him up at the local motel. 'Rustic,' she calls it. So she was wondering—"

I halted in the face of Miss Kellor's steady gaze. "Yes?"

"She was wondering," I said in a sudden rush, "if you could take Brett as a paying guest. For just two nights."

"Oh—uh—" Miss Kellor looked away from me. "I don't think so."

Even though my mind said Miss Kellor had every right to refuse my plea, my heart stung a little. It reminded me of the way my parents used to put off my requests to have a friend stay over.

"You see, Mindi, none of the unoccupied bedrooms are—kept up. They'd be an embarrassment to Lu Ann as well as to me—"

"That's all right," I said quickly. I knew there wasn't a room in Kellor House that would embarrass a person of taste.

"Mindi, dear." Miss Kellor turned to me, concerned. "Please understand; if I could, I'd love to help you out."

"I know you would. Really, it wouldn't hurt Brett to stay in Shawano," I said, naming a larger town fifteen miles down the highway.

I vowed to follow my instincts from now on when it came to delicate situations. And I turned the conversation to our preparations for the big Christmas dinner.

Christmas Eve came in on soft, thick snow. The dining table and a spare were already stretched to their limits and set beautifully for tomorrow's feast. Miss Kellor and I were semi-exhausted from cooking, cleaning, and decorating. So Michael served us supper in the drawing room—mulligatawny, the thick, rich chicken soup his mother had always served on Christmas Eve.

"And sometimes Christmas Day and the day after and the day after," he kidded. "Depending on how many creditors were pounding on the door."

Miss Kellor opened a bottle of her best wine, and the three of us sang Christmas carols to her accompaniment on the out-of-tune grand piano. Then she pleaded fatigue and went to bed early.

Michael and I lazed in front of the cheerful fire to finish off the wine and admire the tree by its own gentle glow.

"This is nice, isn't it, Mindi?" Michael reached from his end of the sofa to take my hand.

I loved the warm, slightly roughened texture of his palm curled around mine. "This is the best," I replied simply. And for me it was.

Michael lifted our clasped hands for a playful brush across my nose. "Even before we open all those interesting-looking packages under the tree?"

I met his soft, mischievous grin with one of my own. "You don't play fair. I notice you've put more presents under there than Miss Kellor or I have. You want us to feel like pikers?"

Michael laughed aloud. "So you've been snooping in the packages, have you? Maybe yours are all sticks and coal."

I stuck my tongue out at him. "Maybe yours is Duck a la Carle."

"Hey! Spare me that and I'll let you have one of your presents early."

This was the opening I'd been looking for. "Fine. Excuse me a minute, and I'll find an early present for you too." I ran upstairs to my room to get Erin's portrait.

When I returned to the drawing room, Michael was standing at one of the big arched windows. Outside, moonlight glimmered on the clean, new snow. It struck me that he looked momentarily—sad. I wondered if he was remembering other Christmases, other times that had included little Erin.

I kept the portrait tucked behind me as I walked toward him.

"I've done something kind of—presumptuous," I began. "I mean—" All of a sudden a thousand doubts swarmed over me. Michael could be an intensely private person. What if he didn't like it that I'd painted Erin's portrait?

He turned toward me. Whatever melancholy he'd been feeling gave way to a welcoming smile. "That's not another petrified duck you're hiding behind you, is it?"

We both laughed. Then I drew the portrait, now in a simple gold-leaf frame, from behind me. Tentatively I handed it to Michael.

The smile left his lips as he studied Erin's likeness. At first I thought he was angry; then I saw tenderness flood his face.

"That's beautiful," he murmured. "How did you remember so well, from just one look at her picture?"

"Oh—I have ways. And I looked at you. The resemblance is remarkable, you know. Except for the nose."

Something in my voice made him look from the portrait into my eyes. "She has her mother's nose," he said at last.

"And her father's hair and eyes and smile?"

Michael moved to study the portrait by the light of a floor lamp near the fireplace. Then his eyes returned to mine. "There's a reason I can't say anything more about Erin, Mindi." He seemed to search for words. "I won't lie to you, and I can't tell you the truth—that is, any more than you've guessed. So, please—"

His words dropped off; we gazed at each other wordlessly. I didn't know whether I felt better or worse, knowing for sure he was Erin's father. Why, *why* couldn't he tell me any more?

"Please don't say anything to anybody about Erin," he finally went on.

"I won't," I answered slowly. "I meant no harm doing the portrait—"

"Mindi!" Swiftly Michael set the portrait on the mantel and came to my side. He took my hands in his

Shadows and Secrets

and looked deep into my troubled eyes. "I don't think you'd ever do harm to anyone. Not deliberately. The portrait is beautiful. It's priceless to me." Tears glinted in his eyes. "Thank you, from the bottom of my heart."

He leaned down to kiss me, a soft, tender touching of lips that thrilled joyously all the way to my heart. His left arm came around me, and he led me to the Christmas tree.

"The little, private gift I got for you—it's nothing compared to Erin's portrait. But I did look a long time for it." He reached carefully between strands of old-fashioned tinsel to a small gold-wrapped package on an inner branch. He handed it to me, and I saw in his eyes the same happiness in giving I'd seen at my impromptu birthday party.

I slid off the elegant wrapping; underneath was a flat jeweler's box. I opened it. The chain gleamed with the rich patina of real gold. On it was a delicate pendant, two hands lifting up a crowned heart.

"It's lovely!" I slipped a forefinger under the pendant.

"It's a claddagh."

I glanced up at Michael inquiringly.

"It's a Gaelic symbol of eternal friendship. Or even—love."

Something within me began to tremble. Carefully I

removed the necklace from its satin bed. I held it toward Michael. "Would you?"

"Gladly." He took it from me, and with typical male clumsiness worked at the tiny clasp until it opened. I held my long hair off my neck and turned while he fastened the chain around my throat.

I turned to face him. I released my hair. It swept over his hands, and I could feel their tremor as they slid up through the warm strands to mold around my face.

"I've never loved a present more," I whispered. "I don't think I'll ever take it off."

"Mindi, Mindi—" Michael's green gaze glowed with tenderness. "I wish I could give you more. Anything you wanted."

He pulled me into his arms, against the beat of his heart. For a few seconds I was lost in the bliss of his lips gently plundering mine.

"I could get used to this," he said with an unsteady chuckle when we came up for air.

"So could I!" I agreed breathlessly.

We kissed again. Reluctantly we stopped.

"I suppose the smart thing for me to do right now would be to say good night?" I murmured.

"Mm-hmm." Michael's lips were browsing over my cheek. "But play dumb for just one second more!"

When I finally forced myself to break away from

his kiss, his muscular arm held me tight to his side as he walked me toward the door.

I dreamed all that night about Michael's kisses, his strong arms, the clean, tangy scent of his skin. Yet sometimes a shadow fell over our fantasy romance—the disturbing shadow of Michael's unknown past.

Chapter Nine

Lu Ann had gone straight from her Chicago date with Brett Campbell to her parents' home in Springfield. So when she called me over to her Sauk Valley apartment two days after Christmas, we had a lot to talk about.

"That's a beautiful tam and scarf you're wearing," Lu Ann said as I came through her door.

"Miss Kellor's gift," I explained as I handed her my coat and the hand-knit cinnamon wool accessories. "You should see the sweater she knit for Michael. Black with a diamond design in teal, gray, and iris. It's a class act!"

"And what have we got here?" Lu Ann cast admiring eyes on the claddagh gleaming around my neck.

I told her about it and about the sophisticated silk scarf and half-dozen other intriguing trinkets Michael had showered on me.

After five minutes I cut off Lu Ann's taunts and romantic insinuations with, "Okay, let's get down to business. How was your evening with Brett Campbell?"

Lu Ann fluffed a hand through her silky blond hair. "Mindi, I'm beginning to wonder why I teach chemistry. Because I sure don't seem to generate a lot of it!"

"Meaning?"

She uttered a wry laugh. "Don't get me wrong—Brett's a fascinating guy. But he's so wound up in his work. I was alone with him for a total of maybe twenty minutes. The rest of the time he was running down stories, fraternizing with the wheels at the party. I was just along for the ride."

"That's too bad, Lu Ann," I commiserated. "So what about New Year's Eve? Did you get a chance to invite him down?"

She nodded. "Who knows? Maybe if I can get him out here to Podunk Junction, I can hold his attention. I mean, what kind of big story is he likely to luck onto in Sauk Valley?"

I chuckled with her over that. "I'm just sorry he couldn't stay at Miss Kellor's."

"Don't worry about that, Min. I'll get him a room

Shadows and Secrets

at the Hotel Shawano. By the way, you and Michael are going to be at the party, aren't you?''

"As far as I know. We've been so busy cleaning up after Miss Kellor's Christmas feast, we really haven't talked about it. Do you have any idea how much table linen, china, crystal, and sterling it takes to serve a five-course sit-down dinner for twenty? We just got the last of it washed, dried, ironed, polished, and put away!''

As I was walking home from Lu Ann's—her apartment was only four blocks from Kellor House—a snowball zoomed out of the twilight and splattered on the sidewalk ahead of me. I whipped around, expecting to catch some errant schoolboy in the act.

"I could have hit you if I'd wanted to, but I didn't want to.''

Michael came trotting up, frosty breath whitening the air around his big grin. The rakish tilt of his red stocking cap emphasized the fun snapping in his eyes and the good health coursing in his veins.

"It's a good thing you didn't want to, Buster! I've got a pretty good throwing arm!''

Michael slowed to a brisk walk and took my hand as we headed together toward Kellor House. He'd been at the high-school gym, playing basketball with some of the faculty men.

"I picked up some news from Coach Charles,'' he

said, "that helps explain Mr. Dikes's touchiness over son Lonny's extracurricular woes."

"Oh?"

"The football game he missed? A recruiter was there from Dikes's college alma mater. Dikes was counting on Lonny getting an athletic scholarship to the school. Instead, Lon missed the game, and the recruiter's eye fell on Lon's teammate, Joe Jensen. Consequently, guess who got an offer from the school?"

"The same Joe Jensen who reigned as King of the Snowball?"

"The same."

"Oh, great! That ought to cement bad relations between Mr. Dikes and me forever!"

"Money and kids—hit someone in either of those touchy spots, and you've got trouble. Hit them in both—" Michael shook his head. "I wouldn't have wanted to be around the Dikes plantation when Ol' Massa got that information!"

"I wonder if *I'll* be around the ol' Sauk Valley School plantation after contract time comes around."

"There are six other members of the school board, Mindi. Dikes doesn't lead them around by the nose. Just keep doing the best you can and take one year at a time."

"Speaking of years," I said, "Lu Ann's wondering if you're going to be at the Simmses' for New Year's Eve."

"Are you?"

"I'm planning on it."

"Then I expect I'll be there too."

My day was made! Lu Ann was right. This year New Year's Eve would be different! This year it would be great!

"Who are they having?" Michael asked. "The usual cast of thousands?"

I answered as he held open the Kellor House kitchen door. "Pretty much so," I said, stepping inside. "With one addition. A new date of Lu Ann's, Brett Campbell."

Miss Kellor came out of the pantry at that moment. "Did I hear you mention your friend, Brett Campbell?" she inquired.

Michael looked from Miss Kellor to me. "Your friend? I thought he was Lu Ann's."

I explained very briefly that I'd known Brett first, but he was especially interested in Lu Ann.

"Yes, Michael," Miss Kellor put in smoothly. "He's a journalist. With the *Chicago Tribune*."

The change that came over Michael in that split second astounded me. The old, tight lines clamped around his eyes and mouth.

"Really? And you know him pretty well?"

Could he be jealous? I was a little offended by his sudden coolness.

"We got acquainted when I was court illustrator for

Kane vs. Kane. He'd just come to the *Tribune*. From Indianapolis, I think it was."

"Oh."

The conversation about Brett dropped right there. Michael went up to his office to do some paperwork—or so he said—and I started preparing yet another after-feast concoction, turkey tetrazzini.

Dinner that night was a bit strained. Not that Michael didn't make an effort to be pleasant. But that was the trouble; it was an effort, not his usual easygoing banter. Miss Kellor's cheerful comments seemed a trifle forced too.

Later that evening I walked into the den and some kind of hushed talk between Michael and Miss Kellor.

". . . shouldn't you tell her?" Miss Kellor was asking.

"I *can't*—"

Michael's reply halted abruptly. The dead-serious expressions evaporated instantly from his and Miss Kellor's faces, but I still felt like an intruder and excused myself as soon as possible.

The next morning Michael called me aside to say he wouldn't be in town for the Simmses' party, after all. "There's an administrators' conference in Springfield January second," he said. "Mr. Whitaker can't go, so I—uh—need to go down a couple days ahead to—do some research."

Research? Over the New Year's holiday? I'd have

Shadows and Secrets 115

laughed in the face of any student who came up with such a ridiculous excuse.

"I've been out of it—administration, I mean—for a while," he stammered in the face of my incredulous stare. "There are a few things I need to—reacquaint myself with."

"I'm sure," I said at last. I was struggling with hurt anger.

"Mindi—" Michael's brows knit in concern. "I'm really sorry this came up. You know I'd rather be with you."

I wheeled and headed toward my room. "No, I don't know," I said and slammed the door behind me.

A few minutes later Zeta met me at the back door as I started for a cool-off walk downtown. "Come on back in, Mindi," she requested. "I can tell all three of you at once what Fred and I have dreamed up for New Year's Eve."

Right at the moment I was soured on the subject, but, of course, there was nothing to do but try to show some enthusiasm as Zeta outlined her plans. She and Fred lived on a farm several miles out of town. Thanks to the unusually cold weather, their pond had frozen smooth as glass for skating.

"And I've always told Fred all those hills surrounding it were good for something," Zeta explained. "So we're going to beg, borrow, or steal every kid's sled we can come upon. If you can't skate, you can sled, or if you don't want to do either, you can sit around the bonfire and sip hot toddies!''

"Zeta, it sounds absolutely delightful," Miss Kellor volunteered in the awkward second following the announcement. "And I hereby offer my services as keeper of the toddy pitcher and stoker of the fire!"

In the laughter that followed, I waited for Michael to announce he couldn't be there. He didn't.

"Just be sure to bundle up," Zeta warned. "Ski masks, if you've got them. The wind whips around the back forty pretty sharp!"

After Zeta left, I went out into the crisp, cold air for my walk downtown. When I returned, Michael beckoned to me as I passed the open door to his home office. He was on the phone; he smiled at me as he signed off on the conversation.

"Mindi, that was Mr. Whitaker. He's decided to make the trip to Springfield, after all, so I'll be here for the Simmses' Snow Fest!"

I couldn't mistake the delight in his eyes. But I could—and did—wonder just what kind of relationship we had that the warmth of Christmas Eve could vanish, then return, at the snap of a mood. For the thousandth time I pondered the conversational fragment I'd picked up between Michael and Miss Kellor in the den:

"... *shouldn't you tell her?*"

"*I can't—*"

Shadows and Secrets   117

Nevertheless I went to the Simmses' party with Michael and Miss Kellor.

The evening was gorgeous. Cold, yes. But a great full moon rose over the silvery surface of the pond and the glistening hillsides weathered to a fine sheen perfect for sledding.

Out of the corner of my eye I kept watching for the arrival of Lu Ann and Brett Campbell. What would Michael do or say when he was introduced to Brett?

As it was, I had to put my curiosity on hold. Between semidarkness and the wild assortment of earflaps, mufflers, and ski masks, it was hard to recognize any one of the fifty-some guests from another.

Fred Simms had dragged a three-sided shed to the pond's edge. Inside that makeshift shelter, Miss Kellor presided over huge thermoses of hot toddy, mulled cider, and cocoa. Outside the shelter, a roaring bonfire cast flickering shadows that did more to hide than illuminate.

Before I knew it, I'd gotten caught up in the fun of the night. No one was better at frolicking like carefree children than a school staff on holiday. The pond was alive with skaters; the hillsides rang with the shouts of sledders. Mr. Whitaker and some of the other men set to work building snow forts from which they pummeled each other unmercifully with snowballs.

"Sheesh! I'd hate to get hit with anything that had the force of his weight behind it!" I cracked to Michael.

"Worse yet, what if he slipped and fell on you?" Michael quipped with a wide grin. "You'd be a grease spot! Come on, let's get out of the line of fire and find a couple of sleds. I haven't been on one since I used to hitch onto bumpers in the back streets of Chicago."

"You didn't sled in the North Woods?"

"Nope. It's all snowmobiles in Minnesota."

The next two hours led me to believe my New Year's Eve jinx had indeed been laid to rest. Michael and I shared a hillside with Coach Charles and his wife, Sue. We slid and laughed and tumbled with the abandon of second-graders. I couldn't think of a time when I'd had more fun.

Then the wind started to come up. Zeta's plan was for us to stay out till eleven o'clock or till we all got frostbitten, whichever came first. Then we'd go into the farmhouse and greet the New Year with her fiery chili and the go-withs brought by guests.

By ten-thirty it was pretty clear that frostbite was the winner. The moon began to hide behind fast-scudding clouds. Snow started to fall. And fall. And fall! Through a thick wall of stinging particles, Fred led the group toward the farmhouse. We could barely see the beam of his flashlight as Michael and I ploughed along with Miss Kellor between us.

Once at the house, we all piled into the basement to shuck our snow gear. Jokes about getting snowbound flew as we moved on into the big recreation room and rubbed cold hands in the cheerful heat of the log-burning stove. The tantalizing vapors steaming from a chili caldron made our mouths water.

It was at this point I sensed a change coming over Michael. The playful attitude of the past two hours was replaced with a well-camouflaged watchfulness. I could guess what was causing it. He was on the lookout for Brett Campbell.

Then I spotted them,. Brett and Lu Ann, in a far corner of the room. I waved at Lu Ann, who tugged at Brett's sleeve to turn his attention our way. Brett waved back, his handsome face lighting up with a big smile. He and Lu Ann started weaving a path toward us.

I turned to Michael—and he was no longer at my side. Across the room, he was helping Fred carry in an ice chest full of champagne bottles.

"Mindi! Good to see you, old girl!" Brett's arm came around my shoulders in a friendly hug. "Say, this is an all-right party! And from the looks of the weather out there, it may go on quite a while."

Lu Ann, Brett, and I chatted for several minutes. Out of the corner of my eye I could see Michael moving around the outskirts of the crowd, talking, laughing, helping Zeta and Fred serve drinks—and always preserving a wide distance between himself and Brett Campbell. I was glad when Mr. Whitaker bumpered up to meet Brett and I could slip away to Michael's side.

"I thought you'd deserted me," I chided lightly.

"Just trying to help out our hosts," Michael replied a shade defensively.

"Oh. Well, if I didn't know better, I'd think you were trying to avoid Brett Campbell."

The outdoor flush in Michael's cheeks deepened. "I've got no problem with him."

I saw Brett leave Lu Ann's side and head straight toward us. "Good. Because here he comes—"

"Zeta! You promised to show me the rest of your house!" Michael took Zeta by the arm and practically dragged her to the stairs. "It's more than a hundred and fifty years old? And part of it was an old stagecoach inn?"

Zeta flung me a mystified look, then led Michael up to the second floor.

That was on purpose, I thought. *Michael is using Zeta to dodge Brett. Now what's going on here?*

I glanced over at Miss Kellor, who was arranging food on the buffet table. She'd apparently observed the whole scene, a worry frown pulling at her brow.

There was nothing for me to do but mingle with the crowd and celebrate as best I could, with half my mind pondering the mysterious shenanigans of Michael J. McCain. The only conclusion I could draw was that he was jealous of my connection to Brett.

Shadows and Secrets 121

It was nearly midnight before I saw Michael come down the stairs. In the meantime Zeta and Fred were making sure everyone had full champagne glasses for the magic moment at twelve.

"Well, you must have found the house fascinating," I said when Michael came to me with our celebratory drinks.

He didn't say anything, just smiled, a preoccupied look in his eye.

"Countdown, everybody!" Zeta called out. Pointing to a clock on the wall, she led us in a chorus of "Ten—nine—eight—seven—six—five—four—three—two—one—Happy New Year!"

Guy Lombardo's schmaltzy "Auld Lang Syne" swelled from the stereo. Glass rims tinkled and lips touched in a salute to the new year. Michael and I shared a chaste peck suitable for public display.

"Later," he murmured, "let's do this lots better!"

Just then Floyd Benson came into the recreation room, his shoulder-length hair and drooping mustache matted with snow. "Hey, man," he announced as he wiped off his John Lennon spectacles, "I just went out to make sure my old Toyota would start, and it's like Yukon City out there! Drifts all over the place."

"You mean, it's not a joke about us being snowbound here?" somebody asked.

"Now, not to worry," Zeta assured us. "We've got a couple of snowmobiles in case anybody's really desperate to go home. Otherwise we might just as well relax and party down!''

I looked at Michael. "Guess we should have brought our jammies," I kidded.

"Yeah. Right," he replied halfheartedly. His glance flicked to Brett Campbell, conversing easily with a group by the stove. As a newcomer—an extremely personable one—Brett was garnering plenty of attention. "It'll be a little—confining, won't it?"

I couldn't place the tone of Michael's remark. Was it discomfort? Or plain old jealousy?

Before I could reply, a very large body swept me into its arms. "There's a space cleared for dancing," Mr. Whitaker boomed, "and rank has its privileges, McCain."

I looked back over my shoulder at Michael as I was half carried away. He grinned and winked, and I suddenly thought of grease spots. I concentrated on not letting Mr. Whitaker turn me into one.

And that was the last I saw of Michael at the party. By the time the music stopped and Mr. Whitaker gallantly bestowed his dancing skills upon Martha Wills, the home ec teacher, I had been ditched. Stranded. Left to my own devices.

At least that's the way it felt when Zeta came up to me and handed me the keys to the Bronco. "Mindi, honey," she said quietly, "Michael had to leave."

"He *what?*"

Shadows and Secrets 123

"Shh! Shh! Don't be upset. He says the furnace has been acting up at Kellor House. Miss Kellor's worried sick it'll shut down and all the water pipes will freeze. So he took one of our snowmobiles and went to check on it."

"He went out in a blinding snowstorm to check on water pipes?" I asked unbelievingly.

Zeta gently shushed me. "Yes," she whispered. "But he asked me not to mention it to anyone but you. Miss Kellor feels bad enough about it as it is."

"Oh, brother!" I huffed. "Don't worry—I won't say anything. People would think he'd gone crazy!"

"Mindi, please." Zeta's hand clamped the top of her head. "I'm already getting a headache just thinking about all these people to feed and bed down for who knows how long!"

"All right, Zeta," I said with grim determination, "I won't blow up right now. But when this party's finally over and we've all gone back to 'normalcy,' you and I are going to have a good, long talk. About Michael J. McCain."

"Right, Mindi. A good, long one."

Unconsciously my hand rose to the claddagh around my neck. Where was the eternal friendship—or even love—it had promised?

"Bummer!" I muttered. Another New Year's Eve. Another bummer. The worst bummer I'd experienced yet.

Chapter Ten

It was a good thing the electricity didn't go out during the big snowstorm. Without the Parade of Roses and other TV diversions, I'm not sure how the Simmses would have coped with the New Year's Eve Party That Would Not Die. It was two-thirty the next afternoon before the township snow plow opened the road to Sauk Valley. The situation that had created a lot of merriment the night before was rather a tired joke by that time.

I drove Miss Kellor home in the Bronco, handed Michael the keys, and went up to my room to get some sleep. I didn't know—or ask—the status of the Kellor House furnace.

School was a day late taking up because so many roads were blocked. When we finally got back in session, I began seeking chances for that good, long talk with Zeta. The Sauk Valley schools were all in one U-shaped building, with all the offices and the two gyms in the center part. Every time I passed Zeta's office on my way between schools, I peeked in. But she was always swamped with work.

At last I caught her during lunch hour. I brought my cafeteria tray to the long table reserved for staff. After a brief exchange of pleasantries, I homed in on the subject that was bothering me.

"Zeta, what was going on at your party? Do you have any idea why Michael made such a big point of avoiding Brett Campbell?"

"No. Why would I?"

"He didn't say or do anything on the house tour to give you a clue?"

"Really, Min, that whole night is just a blur to me. I was so worked up about the storm. I mean, fifty people, two bathrooms, the possibility of being without electricity.... I was justified, Min!"

"What about at the office—you haven't picked up anything that clarifies his background?"

Zeta's jaws clamped around a piece of celery. She avoided my eyes as she bit down and chewed an excessively long time. "Oh . . . he might be a little uptight about strangers coming into the building. He's given me very strict orders to keep them in the office until

Shadows and Secrets

he can check them out. I suppose that's a leftover from his days at Chicago South."

I probed. I prodded. Zeta couldn't—or wouldn't—tell me anything more.

"Look, Mindi," she said at last, "I know you care a lot for Michael. I know there's so much you don't know about him. But no matter how much other people tell you about a man, you'll never know everything about him."

"A few simple facts would suffice at this point, Zeta," I reminded her. "Like why he dropped out of education for two years, why he became a North Woods guide when he doesn't even like shooting animals—"

Zeta's thin, capable hand covered mine. "Mindi, what does your instinct tell you about Michael? I grew up with Fred. We got married after one year of college each. That was twenty years ago. And you know what? I still sometimes have to rely on just my instinct when it comes to Fred, because I don't know all about the man!"

"Zeta—"

Her light hazel eyes pinned mine. "Maybe it's better if things cool off between you and Michael. There's been some talk, you know—just idle chatter—that you two are getting very—close."

I grimaced. "And wouldn't that be just scandalous if it were true!"

"Nobody's suggesting scandal. But, as you say,

Michael's background suggests— Well, maybe it's not wise to get too close to someone in the habit of making sudden changes.''

The bell rang just then, ending the lunch hour. I went to my next class more frustrated than before I'd quizzed Zeta.

Lu Ann came to see me at Kellor House that evening. I was glad. The furnace was working fine, but the atmosphere when Michael and I were in the same room was decidedly chilly. I brushed aside all his attempts to go on as if nothing had gone wrong New Year's Eve.

"Have you heard from Brett?" I asked Lu Ann.

"No. I didn't expect to. He's working on a big assignment. As usual.''

"But you *will* hear from him, won't you?"

Lu Ann laid down the cross-stitchery she'd brought to work on. "I don't know that I want to." To my startled look, she replied, "The problem is, Mindi, there is no Podunk Junction for Brett. Every setting— even a small-town snow party—is just one more story lode for him to mine.''

"Well, he's interested in people."

"Mm-hmm. And that's nice, to a point. But I'd prefer him to be more interested in *me*. Instead, he spent the whole evening at the Simmses' taking life histories, just like he did mine over beer and brats. Oh, he's got all the right hormones! But his idea of a fine relationship is 'story first, girl second!' No thanks!''

I sighed. Sauk Valley was such a nice little town. But as a breeding ground for romance, it was something of a dud.

My personal life may have been on an unpredictable course, but I was beginning to gain some small, solid satisfactions from my teaching career. For one thing, the first-semester dawdlers had spread the word that high-school art courses were no shortcut to an easy A. With smaller but more dedicated classes, I had more time and energy to work toward my major goals for the year.

One goal was to start a high-school art club. My students were enthusiastic when I explained how field trips, visits from outside experts, and the camaraderie of shared interests could add an important dimension to their artistic growth.

We weren't on good terms at Kellor House, but at school Michael and I still communicated at a professional level. Accordingly, I laid my plan before him as the first step in gaining approval for the new club. He took it under advisement, with the promise to get back to me as soon as possible.

In the meantime I worked daily at another prime goal, to show my students how the knowledge of artistic principles could be applied to everyday life. When I found that all the boys in Studio Art II would be absent two days for a special males-only health presentation, I decided to use the time for a subject pretty much exclusive to girls' interests. We'd just started a unit on the basics of portraiture. So the day before the presentation, I asked for a volunteer to help me with an experiment. I would demonstrate the relationship between hue, value, chroma, proportion, and the human face.

In other words—who would be my guinea pig for a cosmetic makeover?

I had plenty of volunteers! I chose shy Alison Carey, the girl I'd persuaded to serve punch at the Snowball because otherwise she'd never have attended.

Alison's parents were divorced, and she lived with her father and three younger brothers in the poorest section of town. She was a good student, but so colorless that kids and teachers alike tended to ignore her. I'd been looking for a chance to bring her more into the light.

Her hair was thin, straight, and too long for her small frame. So the first day, as I talked about proportion, I cut and styled her silvery-blond tresses into a pert, short bob.

Alison didn't have much for clothes. That's when Mom inadvertently became part of the second day's lesson. Mom had been at the bargain table again. My Christmas present from Florida was a cotton-knit sweater in a shade between lilac and violet. It would have been fine—if I had been two sizes smaller and didn't look ghastly in that color! But combined with the right makeup tones, it would work very effectively with Alison's light gray eyes and white skin. We didn't mention to the class that the sweater had been mine and now was hers.

I often played appropriate tapes—usually serious instrumental music—to set the mood for a lesson. For the second session I went lighthearted with Miami Sound Machine. To its soft strains, I busily lectured and at the same time worked some subtle cosmetic magic to liven Alison's features.

The school heating system had a tendency to overdo its duties. Since my studio was the only room in use in that corridor, I usually kept my door wide open to provide a bit of circulation. Just as I added the final touches to Alison's transformation, I glanced into the hallway.

There he was. Mr. Dikes lurked just outside my door. Again. Since the new semester began, I'd seen him cruising the Sauk Valley hallways often, always managing to pause just outside whatever room I was in. The irritated frown now beetling his brow told me all too well what he thought of my present lesson.

On an impulse I walked quickly to the door. "Mr. Dikes, would you like to come in and visit our class?"

"Uh—no! No, thanks!" Harley Dikes turned and strode down the hall.

He's on his way to complain to Michael, I knew instinctively. *With his mindset, he'll be convinced I'm running a beauty salon on school property!*

I turned back to my class. Alison sat, small and still, under the artist's smock I'd put around her to protect her clothing. She tensed in half-fearful expectation as I handed her a large hand mirror.

For a full second Alison studied her reflection. I took the smock from her shoulders. The deep lilac sweater heightened the delicate pinks and violet-grays I'd used on her face.

Nobody said anything; then Marietta Page let out a soft, admiring whistle. Applause grew, and so did Alison's smile.

I looked at that sweet, delighted girl, and I thought, *I don't care if I do get in trouble over this lesson. It was worth it.*

The intercom came on. "Ms. Carle, would you please come to Mr. McCain's office at your earliest convenience?" Zeta asked.

It hadn't taken Mr. Dikes long to lodge his complaint.

The next hour was my planning period. Tensely, I screwed up my nerve and headed for Michael's office.

He looked up from a folder in his hand when I entered. He twirled the pen in his hand—the Christmas present I'd been so happy to give him. "Please, have a seat," he said, indicating a chair. His smile was so very professional, so impersonal, I knew he was about to say something I wouldn't like.

"I'm not sure how to broach this subject, Mindi, but—uh...."

"Mr. Dikes says I've turned my studio into a beauty shop," I finished for him.

He cleared his throat. "Yes. Essentially, that's what he said."

"And of course he considers it more evidence of my incompetence? My featherheaded attitude?"

Michael's brow angled. "As board president, Mr. Dikes considers it his duty to make firsthand observations and evaluations around the school."

My lips pulled into a wry line. "I thought that's what principals and superintendents were supposed to do."

"It is. But the plain fact is, Harley Dikes doesn't trust me to be impartial. He thinks I'm letting you 'goof off'—his elegant term—because I'm interested in you. Personally."

"Oh!" I slapped the arm of my chair. "Well, that's a joke, isn't it?"

Michael's eyes blinked at my vehement reply. "Well, the idea I can't be fair with you is—"

"Please—" I cut in, "could I just tell you what was going on in my studio and then get back to work? Regardless of what Mr. Dikes thinks—on any subject—I do work hard to present meaningful lessons."

"I know." Michael's words were quiet and firm. "So please tell me about the 'beauty shop.'"

I did. Michael listened attentively, nodding his head affirmatively as I explained my motives and the results.

"It sounds to me like a good adaptation to the situation. However—"

Here it comes, I thought. *The downer that follows "However."*

"As your principal," Michael continued, "I think I should urge you to play it conservatively for the next few weeks. At least until next year's contracts come out."

"To appease Mr. Dikes?" I hadn't meant to sound quite so surly.

Michael's face went very formal indeed. "Mindi, you know I'll back you all the way. But you're an untenured teacher handling a brand-new program."

"In other words, I could be let go at the drop of a hat."

"Exactly."

I bit back all the unpleasant things I wanted to say about Harley Dikes and my untenured position. "I suppose I can forget my plans for an art club now?"

"Not at all." Michael rose and came around the desk to where I sat. "I think the club's a good idea. So does Mr. Whitaker. We'll present it for the board's approval at the meeting Monday night."

Shadows and Secrets

I sighed morosely. "Where Harley Dikes will shoot it down. Like a duck." I rose and started for the door.

"Mindi—" Michael's hand on my arm stopped me. His eyes searched mine. "You know you can count on me to be in your corner."

"*Can* I? You won't disappear?"

He flushed, deep, dark red to the roots of his hair. He pulled me by the arm, leading me behind a set of file cabinets that shielded us from any sudden intrusion.

"Mindi, can you pretend for just a minute we're back at Kellor House? On nonprofessional grounds?"

I answered with a questioning glance.

Michael tugged gently at the chain tucked into the neck of my sweater. The hands and heart of the claddagh came out of hiding.

"I can't begin to tell you what your friendship means to me, Mindi," he said in a soft, halting whisper. "I ask your pardon for New Year's Eve—for *anything* I've ever done to upset you. Please let's go out for dinner tonight and be—friends—again."

"I don't know," I murmured, confused. "I don't know what to think about you."

"Trust me, Mindi. Please—*trust* me!"

We went out that night for pizza in nearby Shawano. Then we laughed ourselves silly at one of those appallingly dumb *Ernest* movies. All the way home in the Bronco, Michael kept me pulled close, my head on his shoulder. At the shadowed kitchen door, we kissed with a hungry yearning that shook me to my roots.

There was no way to deny it: I was in love with Michael J. McCain. Once back in my room, I finally admitted the fact. All he had to do was touch me, speak to me gently, look at me with that warm, witty, *caring* gaze I'd known so often B.B.C.—Before Brett Campbell—and I melted. I shoved aside his other persona, the dark, moody, mysterious one.

In love. For twenty-four years I'd waited for this glorious state. But it was precisely because I was a full-grown woman, not a starry-eyed teenager, that I couldn't ignore the blank spaces in my knowledge of Michael. Erin was his child; he'd as much as admitted that. What in the world had brought things to such a pass that he couldn't claim her?

I was tortured with questions about Erin's mother. Did Michael still love her? If so, what was keeping them apart? Or was some beast of an ex-wife making Michael's life a misery?

I'd heard of horrific divorces where spouses fought custody rulings or property settlements with every device in the book. Strange—when I'd heard about that kind of wild carryings-on in the Kane vs. Kane divorce, I'd found it almost amusing. In a disgusting sort of way. Well, I wasn't laughing now.

Shadows and Secrets 137

For the life of me I couldn't believe Michael could be mixed up in anything sordid. Yet. . . .

Restlessly I began a hurried neatening of the newspaper stack I was collecting for the fifth grade's papier-mâché project. I had to know! *I had to know!*

Suddenly it hit me, a way to check into Michael's background. I knew one person with the resources to not only discover things in Michael's history that were part of public record, but to find out the shadowy things, the secret parts.

I searched through my address book till I found the phone number Brett Campbell had given me and I'd never used. I slipped downstairs to the kitchen phone.

Yet, my hand hesitated above the phone. Was I doing the right thing? I forced myself to tap out the numbers. I waited, holding my breath, while the phone burbled once, twice, three times. Maybe he wouldn't answer? I half hoped he wouldn't.

"Campbell speaking."

The receiver jumped against my ear. I managed a half-coherent apology for calling so late.

"The name doesn't ring a bell," Brett said when I'd made my request. "So he must not be an ax murderer. Or a crooked politician—"

"Good night, I know that! He's a wonderful person!"

"Wait a minute—now I remember the name. He's

the principal at Sauk Valley Schools, isn't he? Did the vanishing act from the Simmses' bash."

"He had to leave, yes," I answered stiffly.

Brett's tongue clucked. "So you've gone and done it—fallen in love with your boss? And now you need to know if he's been up to something—"

"I didn't say that, Brett!"

"Didn't need to, sweetheart. It's in your voice. Hey, love is perfectly natural, kid! Even for teachers!"

"Brett, I need only two pieces of information. One: Does Michael J. McCain have a criminal record? And—uh—two—" I paused.

Brett chuckled. "And two: Is there a Mrs. Michael J. McCain? Or Significant Other?" he finished for me.

"Yes. Right." Suddenly I wanted to be off the phone. "That's *all* I need to know."

"Gotcha, Mindi. Just give me a little time, and I'll have some facts for you."

I thanked Brett and hung up. I was upset about what I'd done. So I'd kept my promise to Michael and not mentioned Erin? What right did I have to pry into Michael's life?

The right of self-preservation, a small voice deep inside me answered. *In daydreams, mystery and shadows may be all very romantic. In real life they can break your heart.*

Chapter Eleven

There was no midwinter lull in the Sauk Valley school calendar. January and February fled into March, chased by a storm of basketball tournaments, music and literary contests, and high-school play practice. And, of course, there was the daily round of classes.

I was disappointed when the board tabled my request to start an art club until after contract negotiations were completed. However, I went right ahead with a plan I'd made with the play director. On the two nights of the April play my students would arrange a gallery of their works in the central hall. Art club or no, I wanted my kids to get some recognition.

Meanwhile I waited impatiently to hear from Brett Campbell. Every time the phone rang at Kellor House,

I went through the same thrill-chill routine, wondering if it was Brett and if his report would be good or bad.

He got back to me the first part of February. No, Michael had no criminal record. No, there was no wife or girlfriend lurking in his background. Four years ago, his wife had died of pneumonia. Apparently he'd done no serious dating since.

Mentally I revolved those two bits of requested news for some time. Of course it was a relief to know Michael wasn't into crime. But why was he so silent about Erin's mother? If his wife *was* her mother. I conjured all kinds of scenarios: guilt because he was alive and his wife wasn't, or because he'd been unhappy in marriage, or because his in-laws wanted custody of Erin— Finally I called a halt to my imaginings and decided to trust Michael to tell me the truth when the time was right. Naturally, I assumed the matter was closed as far as Brett was concerned.

On the last Sunday in March, Michael, Miss Kellor, and I chaperoned a junior-high group on an all-day excursion to Abraham Lincoln's home in Springfield. Even though Miss Kellor had been out of the classroom for years, teachers and students still valued her fund of fascinating tidbits about Illinois history.

It was late afternoon when we returned to Kellor House. We hadn't been home long when I answered the jangling hall phone.

"Mindi, I've been trying to reach you all day! Have

Shadows and Secrets 141

you seen today's *Chicago Tribune?*" Zeta Simms's excited yelp almost knocked me off the receiver.

"No. We just got home—"

"Ho-ly Mo-ly! We've got trouble!"

"What are you talking about?"

"Get your hands on a *Trib* and give it to Michael. That hotshot reporter Brett Campbell has done a feature on him. Just take my word for it, Min, Michael needs to see it right away!"

A cold stab of misgiving pierced my heart. I clattered the hall phone back onto its cradle. I ran into the den, where Miss Kellor was just sitting down with a cup of tea and the *Trib*.

"Please—could I see that?" I asked breathlessly. I took the paper from the puzzled Miss Kellor and searched frantically for the article.

Where Are They Now? A New Series by Brett Campbell . . . .

I nearly fainted when I saw the picture accompanying the column. It was Michael; only it didn't look like Michael because his face was contorted with pain. A splotch of blood darkened his shirt front, right under the heart.

The parade never ends . . . the colorful procession of heroes and heavies who are Chicago head-

lines one day, mere faces in the crowd the next. Where do they go? What happens to them when the public spotlight dims?

Remember Michael J. McCain? The handsome young vice-principal of Chicago South won a mayor's citation and Chicago's admiration when he threw himself between two students and a cold-blooded gunman. Where is this hero now?

My hands began to shake. Brett Campbell had betrayed me! I strained to read the gist of the article.

Three years ago Michael had driven a notoriously savage teenage gang from Chicago South. In the process, police had killed the leader, Jeremy Roberts, kid brother of mobster Duke Roberts. Six months later a car swept by the front entrance of the school just as Michael and some students exited. Bullets raked the entrance; only Michael's quick action prevented the death of the two students nearest him. But Michael was shot through the back.

Soon after his recovery, Michael J. McCain, a widower, dropped from sight, leaving his three-year-old daughter with a sister and her family in suburban Palatine.

And where is Michael J. McCain today? Serv-

ing as the well-respected principal of tiny Sauk Valley Community Schools in downstate Illinois.

"What has you so engrossed?"

I whirled around into Michael's amused stare. The fun left his face the minute he saw my perplexed frown. "Mindi—what's wrong?"

"I—I—" I thrust the paper into his hands. "I don't understand. Why have you kept all this a secret? It does nothing but make you look good."

Michael took one look at his own anguished photo, read the first lines, then jumped to the last paragraph. He turned a strange, pale gray. "How did this guy get all this information?" he muttered. Sparks—hot, angry sparks—flashed from his eyes.

"What is it, Michael? What's wrong?" Miss Kellor came quickly to Michael's side.

"Here—right here in black and white—information I've given no one but you and Ralph Jenks! What fool—what *devil*—gave this out to a reporter?"

I was stunned; Miss Kellor's face whitened as she read the feature Michael shoved into her hands.

"Oh, dear! This is dreadful! If what you've told me of Duke Roberts is true—"

"It is! He's a nut! A homicidal maniac! He swore vengeance on me the day his brother died. Not just on me—on my family, everyone connected with me! And now he knows right where to look for me. And, worse yet, for Erin!''

I felt the ground give way beneath my feet; I couldn't speak.

"Oh, Michael!" Miss Kellor whispered. "Who could have talked to that reporter?"

"I don't know," he muttered, pacing away from us. He ran a hand over his hair. "Who hates me that much? Not you or Ralph. I know Zeta has a few suspicions, but would she mention them to Campbell?" He glanced at me. "Mindi knows I have a daughter, but I know I can trust her—"

My mouth worked, but nothing came out.

Michael's face darkened. "That leaves just one person who could have done it. I knew Harley Dikes wanted me out of here, especially after the incidents with Lonny, but I never dreamed he harbored so much resentment. Yet he must be the one who set Campbell on my trail."

"Ohh!"

The exclamation burst from me. I felt two pairs of eyes focus on me.

"Michael," I stammered, "Mr. Dikes didn't do it. I know he didn't—"

Neither Michael nor Miss Kellor said anything. They waited for me to go on.

"I had no idea Brett Campbell would publicize what he found."

Shadows and Secrets 145

"Wait a minute!" Michael's eyes burned into mine. "*You* sicced that irresponsible newshound onto me?"

"I *had* to know!"

If I live to be a hundred, I'll never forget the hurt, the disappointment, the cold anger in Michael's voice. "I asked you to trust me. And this is what I get." His words were like a death sentence to me.

I struggled to answer, but suddenly I was back where I'd started a long time ago. Back in front of my parents, fumbling to express my deep need for their approval. Their unqualified love.

Tears sprang to my eyes; I watched Michael turn away and stride into the center hall. I heard his athletic sprint up the spiral staircase. The happy home, the family, the love and respect I'd shared with Michael and Miss Kellor—the whole dream crashed to shards around my feet.

I wasn't sure what to do. I went up to my room to pace the floor and listen to Michael's tense voice in a series of phone calls. Then Miss Kellor went into his room and they talked briefly. When she came out, she came to my door.

"Mindi, would you help me downstairs? We'll pack some food and other necessities for Michael."

"What—where is he going?" I asked anxiously.

Miss Kellor shook her head. "I don't know. But, please—come help me."

I wasted no time following her downstairs. In the

kitchen she began a swift, efficient gathering of canned goods and other nonperishables, learned through years of helping with Brother Nathan's camping expeditions. Under her expert tutelage I stowed them into two veteran boxes from the safari days. Neither of us had time to talk beyond the necessary instructions.

I was filling a thermos with coffee when Michael came down the back stairs. He carried a hastily packed bag in one hand; my stomach churned at the sight of one of Nathan Kellor's rifles in the other.

"Michael, I have something I want you to take with you," Miss Kellor said. She went into the pantry, and I heard the scrape of a seldom-used drawer. She returned with a small handgun—I didn't know enough about firearms to recognize its type—and handed it, plus a box of ammunition, to Michael.

"Nathan brought this back from Germany after World War II. He gave it to me for protection because he was away so often. I've never used it; I pray you never have to, either."

Michael stared at the gun. "Why, that's a Walther PPK; I can't take it, Miss Kellor. It's a collector's item."

"Nonsense, Michael! It's a piece of metal, valuable only to protect innocent life. I've always kept it cleaned and ready for use on the outside chance—heaven forbid!—it might be needed."

Shadows and Secrets 147

Slowly Michael took the gun. Expertly he checked it. He hesitated.

Miss Kellor handed him the box of ammunition. "You'd better load it, Michael. That rifle would be a little obvious in some situations."

Reluctantly he took the ammunition. Then he gave a brief nod of agreement and loaded the gun.

"Thank you, Miss Kellor. When—if—I can quit running and hiding like a common criminal, you'll have this back."

My face burned; obviously I was the present cause of his running and hiding.

Michael got his Bronco from the carriage house and backed it up to the porch door. I wanted to help him load the heavy safari boxes, but he insisted on doing it himself. He turned from the packed Bronco to face Miss Kellor and me.

"I've made arrangements for Ralph Jenks to come back as temporary principal. The only word he's going to give out is that I was 'suddenly called back to Chicago.' There'll be no mention of Duke Roberts. And no mention that Mindi tipped Brett Campbell off to me."

I tried to get in a few words, but Michael cut me off abruptly with, "The Jenkses want you to come to their place tonight; stay with them a few days till the dust settles here. Please, don't waste any time getting over there."

Miss Kellor stepped to Michael's side. "We won't, of course." She reached on tiptoe to kiss Michael's cheek. "Take care, dear boy. God bless you!"

Michael patted her on the shoulder. He looked at me hesitantly, as if he wanted to say something. Discreetly Miss Kellor left us and went back into the house.

"Michael," I said after an awkward silence, "I'm so sorry things turned out this way. It's my fault, I know. I could go with you, help you find an out-of-the-way place to stay with some of my friends—"

He took my shoulders in a no-nonsense grip. "Mindi, no one—and I mean *no* one—is safe around me now. Chicago's a hundred and thirty miles from here—about a two-hour drive for a maniac like Roberts. I've called the county sheriff and the town cop; they're going to keep an eye on this place. I want you and Miss Kellor to get out of here tonight."

"But, Michael—"

"*Tonight!*" he ground out. "Once word gets out that I'm not in town, it'll be safe for you to come back."

"But where will you go—"

"I don't know for sure. And if I did—" His sentence hung, incomplete. I knew what he meant; if he did know, he'd never tell me. I wasn't to be trusted.

"Michael," I persisted, "I have a lot of friends in

Shadows and Secrets

unusual places, people who could help you. Please, let me—"

" 'Friends'?" he broke in. "Like Campbell? With friends like him, I don't need an enemy."

A sudden rush of anger shook me. Yes, I had caused grievous trouble, but not without purpose. Not without reason. As Michael swung up into the driver's seat, I grabbed the Bronco door.

"Listen," I said, short of breath from combating emotions, "I just want you to answer me one thing. If Erin were my age—and if she were—involved—with a man who had secrets, would you want her to trust him? Blindly?"

He started to open his mouth. Then a perplexed frown clouded his features. Without a word, he turned the key, gunned the motor. I stepped back, and he roared off down the driveway as if the furies pursued.

Chapter Twelve

Sauk Valley buzzed with the news that its new high-school principal was a hero. Everywhere I went, at school or downtown, I met a barrage of questions, most of which I couldn't answer. How did his wife die? When was he bringing his little daughter to live in Sauk Valley? Or at least to visit here? Why had he remained so totally silent about his past, since it was a hero's past?

Most people assumed his sudden absence from the school meant he was in Chicago collecting another medal or preparing for media events. Everyone seemed to take it for granted he'd soon be back to bask in the glory of his renewed fame.

Through it all, I maintained a smiling mask. At least

I didn't have to lie when I said I was just as surprised by Michael J. McCain's history as any other Sauk Valleyan. Or when I said I had no idea what he was doing at the moment.

Miss Kellor and I stayed with the Jenkses for two nights. By then, any Sauk Valleyan who couldn't tell an inquiring stranger Michael J. McCain was out of town for an indeterminate stay would have had to have slept through the past three days.

I put in a call to Brett Campbell and told him straight out what I thought of his treachery, of his using Michael's story for his own gain.

Of course, he didn't consider his series treachery. He was a journalist, he reminded me, a darned good one. He hadn't written one word detrimental to Michael J. McCain.

I didn't dare tell him just how much harm he'd done. It might have been on the front page by the next day.

I was so lonely. Much as I valued Lu Ann's friendship, I found myself avoiding her. She considered the article an invasion of Michael's privacy, the final proof of Brett's consuming passion for "the story." Her probing was insightful; I burned with regret for ever delivering Brett Campbell into her life.

And it was worse dealing with Zeta. Now that it was too late, we had our long, clarifying talk. Michael had her unequivocal loyalty.

"Until she introduced him, Lu Ann didn't tell me

Shadows and Secrets 153

she'd brought a Chicago reporter to our New Year's Eve party," she said. "If I'd known what he was going to do, we'd have stayed outside in our ski masks till our mouths all froze shut. Then no blabbermouth could have spilled enough beans about Michael to set Campbell on the hunt!"

I was in no position to explain the culprit wasn't a "bean spiller"; it was one confused, very-much-in-love woman.

Only with Miss Kellor could I voice my fears—for Michael, Erin, and yes, for Miss Kellor and myself. Every creak of the back stairs, every unidentified groan of an old, old house set my nerves on edge. It was so scary, not having Michael's comforting presence right across the hall.

How had Michael stood it? I marveled. Three years with a murderer on his trail. Where had he found the strength to carry on even a semblance of a normal life—let alone a productive one—knowing destruction might fall on his loved ones, as well as himself, at any moment? I knew now what every smile, every happy instant had cost him.

I kept asking myself, *Why didn't you trust Michael's word? Since that first day, when the two of us stood in Brother Nathan's room discussing Michael's wild appearance, every instinct has told you he's a good, honorable man. So why did you bring Brett Campbell into the act?*

But the answer kept coming back in the form of another question. *Why didn't Michael trust me with the truth?*

On the Friday night following Michael's departure from Kellor House, a raw April wind blustered at the kitchen windows as Miss Kellor and I prepared supper.

"Mindi?" Miss Kellor's gentle hand rested above mine. "If you tear that lettuce into any smaller bits, it'll be confetti!"

"Oh! Sorry!" I jerked my thoughts from their usual painful subject to the salad at hand.

"Why don't we take our soup and salad into the den and eat in front of some mindless TV show?" Miss Kellor suggested. "Maybe we can quit worrying for a few minutes about where Michael is and what he's doing."

"Is that what you're doing too? Worrying about Michael?"

"Of course, dear." Miss Kellor poured hot broccoli-cheese soup into ramekins. "He hasn't been out of my mind since Sunday night." She sprinkled crumbled bacon over the plates of green salad.

I dropped the silverware I was placing on trays. My hands flew to my face. "Oh, Miss Kellor, what have I done to him? We were all getting along so well here together. He loved his work; he and his little girl were safe. What have I done to them?"

Miss Kellor's arm came around my shoulders.

Shadows and Secrets

"Mindi, Mindi, you're not the guilty one in this mess. That psychopath, Duke Roberts—he's the villain."

"But Michael blames me. He hates me for endangering Erin—"

Miss Kellor took my hands from my face. She held them firmly in her warm grip. "Hates you?" Her keen eyes searched mine. "I don't know anybody who hates you, Mindi. Least of all, Michael."

"He has a strange way of showing it. Why didn't he tell me about his past? Because he had no confidence in my common sense. In my integrity!"

Miss Kellor sighed and dropped my hands. "I doubt that's the answer, Mindi. Think what the man had been through by the time he came here. The loss of his wife; right on top of that, the shooting. And then the threats from Roberts started. By phone, by letter—once by a UPS-delivered tape recording!"

"I don't understand. If Michael knew Duke Roberts tried to kill him and was still making threats, why isn't Roberts in prison?"

"Oh, Mindi—if only justice were that simple! Knowing Roberts was guilty and proving it—well, those are two different things. There was a trial, and the man who actually did the shooting is in jail. But Roberts is clever and so savage nobody wants to cross him, so the man wouldn't talk. And Roberts is walking around scot-free."

"Oh! It's so horrible!"

"Michael's first concern was Erin and his sister's family. When it was clear the authorities couldn't help him, he moved them to a safer place. Then, to draw danger as far from them as possible, he went as a guide to the North Woods. He's seen his child only on the arrest occasions since then—never on holidays or special times when Roberts would expect him to be with her. He had the private line put into Brother Nathan's office so he could call his sister at odd hours."

"If only he'd stayed in Minnesota! I'd give up knowing him, if that would keep him safe!"

"We all would, dear. But his family isn't wealthy, and guiding isn't lucrative. So when Ralph Jenks—one of the few Michael dared confide in—fell ill, it seemed like the answer to Michael's prayers. He could partially repay the man he respects as a father. And in tiny, out-of-the-way Sauk Valley, he thought he could support Erin by following the career he loves."

Bitter regret filled my heart. "And then I ruined it."

"Mindi, dear, when I saw how things were going between you two—how you were going to be hurt sooner or later—I tried to convince Michael to tell you everything. But the turmoil he'd suffered—he couldn't bring himself to do it. He just wanted to cherish a relationship—a situation—that made him happy."

"You think he was happy? Here in Sauk Valley, I mean."

Miss Kellor smiled sadly. "Oh, yes, Mindi. I think

he'd have been happy in Timbuktu, if that's where he'd met you."

That did it! The tears started afresh, and Miss Kellor patted my back soothingly until I could stop crying and grope for a tissue.

"Let's go into the den and have our supper, Mindi," she suggested. "After a little warm soup and an experience I want to relate, you may feel better."

It was easy to find a mindless TV show to accompany our simple meal. Miss Kellor was right; a few sips of soup and a nibble of green salad did make me feel better. After we'd finished eating, she turned off the TV, and we sat quietly, listening to the wind howling and the windows rattling.

Finally I said, "You were going to tell me something?"

Miss Kellor nodded slowly. "Yes, dear. Something I've told no one else since it happened."

She rose and stood examining a beautiful little figurine on the fireplace mantel.

"A long time ago—I hate to admit how long!—I was in love, Mindi." She turned to face me. "My youth was very privileged. I used to spend my winters in California. And, of course, I met a man on the beach. Oh, I'd experienced the usual resort flirtations, infatuations. But this time it was different. This time I fell blindly, heedlessly in love."

Miss Kellor removed an antique fan from the mantel

and tapped it absentmindedly against her palm. "He wasn't just tall, dark, and excruciatingly handsome; he was well-educated—an engineer—and well-read. We soon found we liked so many of the same things. I lived in a fool's paradise; then Brother Nathan came out to visit me."

Miss Kellor chuckled humorlessly. "You've heard the expression, 'It takes one to know one'? Well, Brother Nathan was rather well-acquainted with—dalliance. He started asking questions—the ones I hadn't asked because I was afraid of the answers. And he brought to light one small fact that had escaped my notice. The man I loved already had a wife. And two children."

Miss Kellor shook her head, her eyes closed. "I did the expected thing; I immediately broke off the romance. And then I turned against Nathan. I said bitter, hurtful things to him, blaming him for my own blindness."

She opened her eyes to focus on me. "I know Sauk Valley finds my loyalty to Nathan Kellor a mystery. I know I'm considered blind to his faults. But what nobody knows is how he stood by me in those awful days, how he let me vent my rage on him, then quietly packed me up and brought me home with never a word about my own foolishness."

Miss Kellor smiled in fond remembrance of her brother. "Eventually I got myself together, started a career I came to love, teaching social studies in the Sauk Valley system. And I grew to love my brother with all my heart. Not because I was blind to his faults, but because he was bigger than all of them."

I was deeply moved by Miss Kellor's story. Knowing her natural pride and reserve, I was touched that she'd reach out to me through an event so painful.

"You're saying, then, I was right to check Michael's background?"

"You were wiser than I was at your age, Mindi. You see, my young man, like Michael, had all kinds of fine qualities. And he didn't start out to be unfaithful to his wife. The attraction between us just came along at a time when they were having difficulties. But it didn't excuse either of us from hiding from the truth."

Our absorption in her story was broken by a startling rap of the great brass front-door knocker. Neither of us moved for a second.

"I'll get it," I said over the pulse of fear leaping in my throat.

"No, I'll go," Miss Kellor insisted. "You stay by the hall phone with your finger on the sheriff's number—just in case!"

I did just that while Miss Kellor turned on the outside light and peeped out a side window.

"Good heavens! What's Harley Dikes doing here?"

For once in my life I breathed a sigh of relief at the

name Harley Dikes. It had a much better ring to it than Duke Roberts!

Miss Kellor opened the door, and Dikes swept in on a gust of cold wind.

"Sorry to bother you, Miss Kellor," he boomed, "but there's a matter I need to discuss with you." He saw me standing behind her at the phone. " 'Evening, Ms. Carle."

I murmured hello.

Miss Kellor showed him into the den. As I stood uncertainly at the doorway, she motioned me to come in too.

"Uh—Miss Kellor," Dikes said, clearing his throat, "I've just come from Ralph Jenks. A matter I've been asked—to keep very private?" His brows rose. "Concerning McCain?"

"It's all right," Miss Kellor assured him. "Mindi now knows the full story too."

With her innate courtesy, Miss Kellor ensconced Dikes on the sofa, and we both took chairs to hear what he had to say.

"I'll come right to the point," he said. "I'm getting hit with a lot of questions about the Honorable Michael J. McCain. Like, 'Where is he? When is he coming back? And why was the sheriff prowling around Kellor House in an unmarked car for a couple of days after McCain left?' So I took it up with Ralph. Finally he came clean."

Shadows and Secrets 161

"Well, the curiosity is understandable," Miss Kellor responded diplomatically.

"It sure is. I gave my word to keep quiet about the killer on McCain's trail. Still, I'm scared this creep Roberts might come into Sauk Valley Schools and shoot up some more innocent people!"

"Do you or Ralph have a solution?" Miss Kellor asked worriedly.

"Maybe a partial one. The school board meets Monday night to evaluate Whitaker and McCain. If they approve the way they've been handling their jobs—and I can tell I'm the only one who might not—the board will offer them contracts for the next year. But—" Dikes gave his knee a resounding slap. "How can we rehire a man who's disappeared into thin air? And may have to stay disappeared for a long time?"

"That is a problem," Miss Kellor agreed.

"You better believe it's a problem!" Dikes affirmed. "Since I can't tell the board the truth, I've got to get in touch with McCain. If he'd send a letter stating his 'emergency' situation makes it impossible for him to finish out this year, Ralph Jenks would handle the last three months of school. The whole affair would soon die down, and the board could go about its business and get a new principal for next year. So, I'm asking you, Miss Kellor, do you have any idea where McCain is?"

"I do not," she answered promptly. "And if I did,

I'd never risk Michael's life by giving out the information."

Surprisingly Dikes nodded his head in understanding. "I don't want to put him in any more danger than he's already in, either. But look at it this way: The longer no one hears from him, the more speculation there'll be. The more people talk, the greater the chance that Chicago hoodlum will pick up some bit of information that might lead to McCain."

Miss Kellor and I glanced at each other. I could tell what she was thinking: For once, Harley Dikes's analysis was correct.

"I'm sorry, Harley," Miss Kellor said. "I don't know where Michael is. It's possible he's back in the Minnesota woods."

"How about you?" Harley Dikes turned sudden, sharp eyes on me. "Have you got a clue?"

All my life I'd been told I had an unusually open face. Under Dikes's shrewd glance I was glad I could truthfully say, "No, I don't."

Dikes sighed heavily and rubbed a hand over his chin. "Well, this is one fine mess—"

The hall phone rang across his remarks.

"Excuse me," I said. "That's probably Lu Ann. She said she was going to call me tonight." I slipped out to the hall phone.

"Mindi?"

My breath caught. "Michael?" I whispered, choked with relief. "Where are you? Are you all right?"

"I'm fine, Mindi. And safe enough for the time being. I checked on Erin earlier, and she's been moved to a safer place too."

"Oh, thank God! Thank God! I've been out of my mind worrying about you—"

"Mindi, honey," he broke in, alarmed, "what's the matter? I can barely hear you. Is someone there?"

"Mr. Dikes. He's in the den with Miss Kellor."

Michael's sigh was quick and relieved. "Okay, hon. No need to tell you who I was afraid it might be. Listen, I've got to keep this real short. But I can't take the chance that something might happen and you'd never know this: I love you, Mindi. I've loved you since that first day when you handed me your lemonade. I love you so much, it tears me up over the way we parted."

"Oh, Michael!" Between joy and fear I could hardly speak. "I love you! If only I hadn't asked Brett Campbell for help! If only I'd trusted you!"

"No, Mindi." Michael's voice roughened with tenderness. "I lashed out at you because—because—the wonderful thing building between us was blasted. But what you said about Erin falling in love someday, trusting some man too much—you were absolutely right. It brought me to my senses."

"But I've exposed you to so much danger!"

"Honey, it was bound to happen sooner or later. I

was a fool to think you and Erin and I could have a good life together as long as Duke Roberts walks around free."

"But what will you do? Please, Michael! Let me come to you!"

"No way! Right now I'm holding on to the fact you and Erin are safe."

"But how long is this going to go on? If I thought I was never going to see you again—"

"Mindi, love—stay calm. Now that I know you and Erin are safe, I'm going to surface. I'm going to end this cat-and-mouse game. I don't want anyone else around when Roberts finds me—"

A sudden burst of noise drowned out Michael's words. It sounded as if somebody had opened a door between him and a boisterous party.

"Oh—sorry, buddy! I thought this was the men's room—" A loud rumble, then a *thwok!*

I knew where Michael was! The Duck Inn! He must be holing up at Nathan Kellor's hunting lodge!

"Mindi—baby—remember what I said. I love you! Stay right there in Sauk Valley till this thing's settled. And when it is—will you marry me?"

"Oh, yes! Yes!"

"It'll happen, Mindi!" *Clack!* The phone went silent.

"Thanks all the same, Miss Kellor," Harley Dikes said, coming out of the den. "I'll have coffee another time. Right now I've got to get over to the school and pick up Lonny from indoor track practice." He fixed me with a meaningful stare. "He's an all-around athlete, you know."

The blunt dig was lost on me. At that moment my thoughts and fears were a wild jumble. The specter of Michael facing down Duke Roberts sent chills down my spine. Michael was an expert game hunter; Roberts was a crazed hunter of men, a killer full of hate. Now that I knew where Michael was, shouldn't I race to him, try to persuade him to lie low?

"I—uh—I'm going over to Lu Ann's for a while," I told Miss Kellor and started upstairs to get my coat. I had no idea where I was going, but I felt like I had to get out of the house, clear my head with a drive—somewhere. I honestly didn't know which was right—to obey Michael, or to follow my own instinct to run to him.

I put on an all-weather jacket and a rain scarf—I could hear drops splashing against the windows now—and ran down the back stairs. I slipped out the kitchen door and paused to let my eyes adjust to the pitch-darkness. I started my first step toward the carriage house and stopped short. There was an odor—like expensive after-shave, but somehow rank. As if it were mixed with sick skin—

"Ahh-h-h!"

A cold, hard hand had clamped over my shriek. Another hand twisted my right arm behind me, jerking me against the man behind me.

Panic tore through me. I knew who this had to be: Duke Roberts! I tried to lurch away from him, but all I got was a wrenched arm.

"Don't make it tough on yourself," a harsh voice muttered at my ear. "I want some information."

The mobster took his hand from my mouth. As I spluttered against the ugly leather taste left by his glove, the kitchen door swung open.

"Mindi?" Miss Kellor peered anxiously into the dark. "Did I hear you call out?"

Miss Kellor gasped as Roberts swung me around to face her. "Come out here, lady," he ordered, "and keep your voice down, or both of you are gonna get hurt."

I struggled again, desperate to break out of his grip. He grasped my long hair tumbling from beneath my scarf and yanked my head up and back. In a sudden flash of lightning I stared into the hard eyes, the cruel, contemptuous mouth above me. And I knew: This was the face of evil!

Chapter Thirteen

"Okay, girl, drive!"

Roberts had forced Miss Kellor and me out to the carriage house and into my old Escort with orders to take him to Michael. Now he crouched on the floor behind the front seat. A wave of nausea washed over me as the sickening odor of his after-shave permeated the whole car.

"We've told you, we don't know where Michael is," Miss Kellor protested.

The menacing blue snout of a pistol appeared between the two front seats, aimed right at her temple.

"THINK...REAL...HARD!"

His warning snarl convinced me. We were dealing with a psychopath who'd think nothing of destroying either of us. I slipped the car into gear and crept out of the carriage house. Ahead of me, Harley Dikes's red pickup was pulling out of the drive.

Oh, Mr. Dikes, I grieved, *why couldn't you have lingered in the drive just a few seconds longer? Maybe I could have given you some kind of signal that something was wrong as I drove up behind you.*

As it was, I delayed too long at the end of the drive to suit Roberts; he jammed the pistol behind my right ear.

"Listen, girlfriend, you try anything funny, and both you and the old lady will be tomorrow's headlines! Now, MOVE!"

"Okay, okay! But I've only been over the road we're going to take once. I'm trying to remember—"

One word describes the winding journey we made that rain-swept night toward the lodge on the Illinois River: nightmare. My mind rocketed between trying to choose the right roads and trying to form any possible way to foil Roberts's plans. I had no doubt that he intended to kill Miss Kellor and me, as well as Michael, and enjoy doing it.

I considered hitting the gas pedal and swerving off the road into a ditch or tree, anything to prevent Roberts from getting at Michael. But I wasn't the only one caught in this death trap with the mobster. Frightened though I was, my heart ached for Miss Kellor. She sat pressed against the seat back, her hands clenched. All

Shadows and Secrets 169

she had on for warmth was the pink sweater I'd given her for Christmas. Shivers racked her stiffened frame.

Thanks to the bad weather and my nervousness, it took nearly an hour to drive the thirty miles to the river. A few miles out of Sauk Valley, Roberts sat up in the backseat. Soon after, a vehicle came up behind us, and I searched desperately for some way to attract the driver's attention to our plight. However, the lights behind us soon veered off onto a side road.

Eventually we made the final turn into the lane below Nathan Kellor's lodge. Above us the lodge sat in darkness. My heart raced; maybe Michael hadn't come back here from the Duck Inn. Maybe he'd changed his mind and decided to move to another place of safety instead of coming up against the thug behind me. I hoped so; at least one of us three victims might be spared.

Roberts stared through the windshield. "Wait a minute!" he growled. "What are you trying to pull? Where's the house?"

"It's up there," I said, gesturing toward the top of the rocky incline. "But I don't see any signs of life; Michael must not be there."

Roberts emitted a short laugh. "You don't think he's gonna make this easy, do you? Prance around with the lights on?"

He produced a flashlight and thrust it into my hand. "Get out," he ordered. "Use this to see your way up that hill. Keep calling out to McCain, and we'll soon find out if he's there. And remember, I'll be behind you. With the old lady."

I got out, slamming the door as hard as I could, hoping that if Michael were there, he'd hear it and take warning.

Roberts was clever. He slid out on the side opposite the lodge, opened Miss Kellor's door, and crouched to pull her out so no momentary light from the dome would reveal him.

"Okay, march!" he hissed at us.

We started our strained procession up the hill. The stony path was so slippery, I fell almost immediately; I was too scared to feel the pain in my bludgeoned kneecaps. Roberts cursed softly and nudged me to my feet with the tip of his pistol.

Halfway up, he announced, "Start calling out to McCain. If he opens the door, shine that flashlight right in his eyes."

My first attempt was a faltering croak, lost in the wind and rain.

"Louder!" Roberts commanded.

I tried again, and then a third time. Not a sign of life from the lodge.

Suddenly Miss Kellor let out a muffled yelp of pain.

"Now, turn up the volume and get that jerk out here, or we'll let Grandma do the calling!"

"You sick animal!" I shouted and turned to see Miss

Kellor with her arm twisted behind her back just as Roberts had done to me at the carriage house.

Grimacing with pain, she gasped, "Don't call out, Mindi!"

Roberts yanked her arm upward. "Yell!" he ground out.

I hesitated a fraction of a second; Miss Kellor couldn't stop a whimper.

"Michael!" I screamed. "Michael! It's me, Mindi!"

There was one long, silent pause; then I heard a door creak.

"The light, fool!" Roberts snarled and grabbed my arm to focus the flashlight's beam on the man at the door. Michael threw up a hand to ward off the glare.

"Mindi! I told you not to come—"

A rough chortle broke from Roberts. "Guess what, McCain? She's not alone!"

I saw Michael's start of disbelief. "Who's with you?" he demanded.

"It's just a bunch of friends, McCain," Roberts mocked. He dragged Miss Kellor forward, then grabbed my arm just long enough to shine the flashlight briefly over the three of us. "See, new friends from Sauk Valley, and me—your old friend from Chicago."

The stunned horror in Michael's face seared my eyes.

"Roberts, you harm one hair on either head, and I'll kill you!"

Roberts uttered a scornful oath. "McCain, you aren't in much of a position to lay down conditions, are you? Now, that gun you're packin' behind your back—throw it out. Right on the deck."

Michael remained motionless. Miss Kellor's breath snagged with pain.

"Don't make me get really nasty, McCain!" Roberts threatened.

Grim lines hardened in Michael's face. Even by flashlight I could see the old stitches whitening above his left eye. But he brought his hidden hand forward. The Walther PPK clunked to the deck floor.

"Come on," Roberts commanded me with a poke of the pistol in my back, "let's all get together, out of the rain."

Once we reached the deck, Roberts picked up Michael's gun and slipped it into his pocket. Then he waved us into the lodge. "Light that lamp," he told me, pointing to the kerosene lamp over the table.

Under its dim glow I saw how wiry he was and filled with coiled energy. Somehow it was more terrible that his thin facial features were rather handsome. If you'd met him on the street, you'd never have guessed he was a killer. Unless you looked into his eyes, where the madness lurked.

"All three of you," Roberts ordered, "get over there against the wall, opposite the door."

My knees were so weak, I could hardly move. This

couldn't be happening; three innocent people weren't about to be blasted into their graves by this sick monster.

"Now, Mr. High-and-Mighty Hero," Roberts grated to Michael as we clustered opposite him, "you're gonna pay for what happened to my brother. You're gonna see these two cut down right before your eyes. And then it'll be your turn."

"This is insane!" Miss Kellor managed in a hoarse whisper. "All the local authorities are looking for you—"

Roberts turned on her derisively. "You think I'm some kind of amateur? I got McCain once, and 'Chicago's finest' couldn't lay a hand on me! You think some two-bit hick cops are gonna do better?"

His manner turned slier, more sinister. "And I'll tell you something else. When I'm finished here, I'll find little Miss Erin McCain. Oh, it won't be easy," he asserted over Michael's outraged exclamation, "like it was in Sauk Valley. I won't be able to pose as a parts salesman and listen to the boys down at the local gas station chat it up about the new town hero. And the old gal who took him in like a son. And the pretty art teacher who's got a real case on him. But I'll find a way. In the meantime. . . ."

Roberts blew imaginary smoke off the tip of the gun. "First things first. . . ."

All my senses seemed to burst onto acute alert. The reek of kerosene and the faint aroma of a past meal clashed with the gaggy rancid odor of Roberts's aftershave. The rain drummed on the roof, almost knocking out the roar of my own blood in my ears.

Outside, lightning flashed. And in one mad moment I thought I'd gone completely crazy. I thought I saw a familiar moon-face peering in through the window on the deck. I thought I saw Harley Dikes!

"Roberts," Michael rasped, "let these two women go." His face was plaster-white and strained. "They haven't done anything to hurt you. I'm the one you want." He took a step toward the gunman.

"Get back, McCain," Roberts snapped. He pointed the gun directly at my head. "I told you—you're gonna watch what happens to these two before I drop you. You're gonna pay for what happened to my kid brother!"

"You're a little late getting concerned about your brother, Roberts," Michael countered. I could see he was scraping for something, anything to gain a little time to find a way out of this horror. "You really cared about him, didn't you, when you set him up as a junior drug lord?"

Roberts flared in anger. "My brother was a great kid! He'd have been a big man on the streets someday—just like I am—but you got him killed!"

"Oh, sure!" Michael scoffed. "He'd have been a big man! Big and dead. Killed either by the cops or his own kind. That's what you set him up for."

Shadows and Secrets

Roberts reached up and unhooked the kerosene lantern from above the table and held it near his jaw. With the light streaming up from beneath his chin, all I could see was a sleek, deadly cobra, floating disembodied before our eyes.

"Look at me! *Look...at...me!*" he demanded. "Am I dead? I started young, and no cops and none of my 'own kind' have been able to put me away. And they never will."

Michael eyed him up and down. "You're gutless. You don't have the nerve to let these two go and fight me one-on-one."

"Fight you?" Roberts's head fell back in an incredulous snort. "You sound like a B movie!" His head jerked forward, and he fixed Michael with a malevolent stare. "I don't play by Boy Scout rules. That's why I'll still be alive after you're dead." His whisper was filled with rage and hate. "And I'm not gonna waste any more time before starting the fun."

Roberts set the lamp back on the table; he glided up in front of me, slowly, treacherously. He placed the dead, cold pistol muzzle right in the center of my forehead. A slow, hate-filled smile spread across his thin lips.

Miss Kellor's hands flew to cover a moan; she slumped to the floor.

In that moment the terror that had grown in me to the point of agony clamped to a stranglehold. Then— shattered! In its place was a white-hot determination.

If I had to die, my death was going to buy a chance for Michael and Miss Kellor.

In the instant that Roberts's trigger finger began to squeeze, my arm shot up to strike the gun aside; I threw myself against Roberts, my left ear ringing with the explosion of the gun right beside it. At the same time, Michael leaped behind the criminal and grabbed at his wrists.

There were no screams, no shouts, just the harsh, jagged breathing of three people locked in a death struggle.

"Mindi!" Michael panted, hauling Roberts back from me, "get out of here!"

I scrambled to pull Miss Kellor with me. Just as I reached her, Roberts tore loose from Michael's grip. Fast as a snake, he whipped to the other side of the table.

"Down!" Michael shouted and threw himself over me, knocking me to the floor. A shot shrieked over our heads as Michael scrambled to his knees, headed for Roberts.

Roberts grasped the gun in two shaking hands; a stream of obscenities spewed from his mouth as he aimed at Michael, still on his knees at the end of the table. His finger clenched around the trigger.

But in that same split second, a bullet ripped through the lamp and struck the gun from Roberts's hands. A geyser of flames shot up and out from the table.

"Don't move, Roberts! You're under arrest!"

Through a splintered door, men—I couldn't tell how many—burst into the room.

Roberts whirled on them; he lost his balance and crashed backward into the inferno raging across the table. His bellows were horrible as he lunged blindly for the door. He stumbled onto the deck, arms flailing as he tried to separate himself from the flames searing his back. For one deathly second he was an agonized silhouette stretching for mercy at the deck rail overhanging the cliff. Then he fell back; the rail shuddered and gave way in one long, decisive *cr-a-a-ck!* . . .

When it was all over, when the deputies had confirmed Roberts was dead on the rocks below, Miss Kellor and I huddled in the backseat of the sheriff's car. On the hill above us flames licked out the lodge windows, hissing and spitting in the rain.

Suddenly I began to tremble; I couldn't stop shaking as the events of the past hour raced before my mind's eye.

Just then Michael opened the car door and slid in beside me. "It's all right, baby," he crooned, pulling me into his arms. "It's all right. Nothing's going to hurt you now."

"Oh, Michael," I whispered, "thank heavens that creature is dead!"

"Amen to that, honey," he agreed. "It's a good thing Harley Dikes showed up when he did—and that he's a crack shot with that rifle!"

A tall, heavyset figure came toward us out of the dark, followed by an equally tall but younger man. Harley Dikes leaned in through Miss Kellor's window. She was already swathed in his down-filled hunting jacket, and I wore son Lonny's. I studied the round face and squinty eyes I'd always considered ugly. I glanced at Lonny's Elvis hairdo wilting in the rain. As far as I was concerned, I was looking at two angels.

"Miss Kellor," Dikes said, "I still think you ought to let us take you by the hospital and get checked out. You've been through a terrible ordeal."

"Thank you, Harley, but no," Miss Kellor replied. "Actually, the worst harm of all was to my dignity. If I never hear the term 'old lady' again, it'll be too soon!"

We all chuckled a bit, glad for Miss Kellor's resilience.

"What about that fainting spell?" Dikes inquired. "When you fell to the floor, my first thought was 'heart attack.'"

"That was just a last-ditch effort to distract Roberts," Miss Kellor explained.

"Mr. Dikes," I said, "you saved us. How did you know to come here?"

The big man leaned in closer to talk to me. "I thought something was up when you got that phone call at Miss Kellor's. Your face gave you away. So I hung around the end of the drive till I saw your car lights coming. When I noticed you and Miss Kellor headed out of town instead of toward Ms. Mobley's, I quick picked up Lonny, then hiked after you to see what was up. About two miles out of town we caught up with your car, and lo and behold, there was a man's head showing in the backseat."

"Dad said he knew pretty well that whatever was happening, it probably wasn't good," Lonny put in. "So we swung off onto a side road and radioed the sheriff."

"We could still see your car lights from where we were," Mr. Dikes continued. "By the time you made a couple of turns, we guessed where you were going. We took a shortcut and got here to the lodge ahead of you."

"But there's just the one lane through the cornfield to the lodge," Michael said. "I saw only one set of headlights turn in here."

"Dad knows a lot about reconnoitering, Mr. McCain," Lonny said with quiet pride. "We turned into the lane with no lights. We'd just gotten the truck hidden back in the cornstalks when Ms. Carle drove in. Dad told me to wait at the head of the lane for the sheriff, and he slipped up on the place by foot. Good thing he always carries his deer rifle stashed in the truck's gun rack!"

"You can say that again, Lonny!" Michael agreed. "If your dad hadn't shot that gun out of Roberts's hand, all three of us might be dead now."

Mr. Dikes's shoulders twitched in an embarrassed

shrug. "I just did what you'd do—what any man would do—in the same situation."

Suddenly he swung around to face the lodge. "Well," he said gruffly, "would you look at that place burn! Dang it all, I've been wanting that lodge for the Sportsmen's Club for years! Ever since Lonny here started showing a real interest in a *man's* hobby—hunting! You know—" He swung back to face us, a perplexed frown creasing his forehead. "Out of all this fracas, the thing I can't believe is a fine, upstanding lady like you, Miss Kellor, lying to me. Looking me right in the eye and swearing you didn't know where McCain was. Why, when I was in school, you'd have sat a kid in the corner for *years* for a fib like that!"

Michael shook his head. "She didn't lie. She never asked, and I never said where I was going—although I'm sure she had a good idea." He turned to Miss Kellor. "It was like the unlocked gun cabinets. Remember, when I first got to Kellor House? You never said, 'There are the guns in case you need them.' But after I got to know you, I realized that's what you meant."

"So you hung onto this place," Dikes wondered aloud to Miss Kellor, "so McCain would have a place to hide out if he needed it?"

"It crossed my mind, yes," she replied.

"Then," Dikes mused, "now that this mess is settled, maybe you'll still sell the land to the Sportsmen's Club?"

Shadows and Secrets

"Gladly, Harley," she said, "and it'll be small thanks indeed for what you did for us tonight!"

The sheriff came out of the glare of work lights and opened the door on Michael's side. "Mr. McCain, we've got to get statements from all of you; then you'll be free to go."

"Fine," Michael said. "Let's do it."

Mr. Dikes and Lonny started to move toward a deputy with an official-looking paper in hand.

"Mr. Dikes—" On impulse, I jumped out of the car and stood on shaky legs. "I just want you to know—" My voice got shaky too. In spite of my best efforts, tears brimmed and I could hardly go on. "You and Lon are so brave. I just wanted you to know, I think you're heroes."

Neither Dikes said anything for a second. Then the big, rough hand of Harley Dikes reached for mine. "Well, you're a mighty spunky girl yourself, Ms. Carle. Knocking Roberts's arm aside and throwing yourself at him. That's what gave me the chance to shoot the gun out of his hands without hitting one of you captives."

The tears spilled out of my eyes, right onto Harley Dikes's big hand. "I wasn't thinking brave. I just did what came naturally."

"Well—now—uh—" Dikes gave my hand a firm squeeze. "Ms. Carle, it's no secret I've been opposed to art—and—uh—frankly, even to *you*—coming into the

Sauk Valley system. But after what I saw tonight—"
He shook his head. "I still don't know how important it is for kids to have art. But they do need a teacher like you to set 'em a good example. Help 'em grow up decent and strong. And you, too, McCain—" He reached to shake Michael's hand. "You know how to handle yourself in a bad situation too."

He gave my shoulder a pat, then began to bustle around to hide the embarrassment it caused him to admit to admiration.

When all the paperwork had been completed, Lonny Dikes took Miss Kellor back to Sauk Valley in my Escort. And Michael took me to where he'd kept the Bronco parked out of sight. For a second we stood facing each other, wordless with relief. Then he folded me into his arms, my face pressed into his warm, strong neck.

"Mindi! Mindi!" he breathed at my ear. "I love you so!"

My response was smothered in a long, committing kiss.

Chapter Fourteen

The scent of roses floated everywhere. On this first day of June, I stood at the head of the Kellor House staircase watching Lu Ann, radiant in yellow linen, take the arm of the best man, Ralph Jenks, and move down the center hall to the drawing room.

"All right, honey," I whispered to Erin. "It's time for you."

Michael's beautiful little girl glanced up at me, a shy, questioning smile on her lips. "And drop the rose petals for you to walk on?" she asked.

"That's right, darling. You walk down the stairs and right to Daddy in the big, fancy room." I stooped to hug my soon-to-be daughter. Erin and I had become great friends in the ever-longer visits she'd been paying to Kellor House. She started down the staircase, sprinkling petals, a confection in yellow organdy.

I drew a calming breath. *Was* everything ready for this wedding Miss Kellor, Lu Ann, and Michael's sister, Sheila, had helped me plan? So much had happened in the past two months. There was the inquest into Roberts's death. Then Michael and I each signed new contracts with Sauk Valley Community Schools. I got my art club and got it off and running for next year. School rushed to its final hurrah the last of May . . . .

The newly tuned grand piano chorded the grand introduction to the bride's march. I started down the stairs, breathing in the delightful scent from the garlands festooning the handrail. At the bottom step, my father—yes, my *father!*—waited to take me to Michael. The terrible Roberts affair had shocked my parents into full awareness that I was part of them, that they wanted me in their lives just as I wanted them in mine. I was so glad.

Now the hem of my midcalf white linen gown, inset with rows of hand-crocheted lace, brushed against the bottom step. I took my father's arm and we started toward the drawing room.

Then it struck—one instant of pure panic. What was I doing? Who was I to take on the vital, yet so delicate task of melding Michael, Erin, and me into a family? Gently weaning Erin from the people who'd loved and raised her?

Shadows and Secrets

We reached the drawing-room door. The room overflowed with friends, including Mr. and Mrs. Harley Dikes and all the others who'd taken me into their lives, given me a secure place in their hearts.

Before the flower-bedecked fireplace, Michael waited for me.

Waited? No. He was coming toward me, his eyes full of love.

Joyously, my heart broke, once and for all, out of the shadows.

I, of all people, knew that "family" wasn't just blood relationship. It was the coming together of any group who wanted, more than anything else, to belong to one another. Michael, Erin, and I—we'd find our way together.

Michael touched the claddagh gleaming at my throat. "Forever, Mindi!" he whispered.

We stepped into the sunshine ringing the fireplace.

"Forever, Michael!"

SANDUSKY LIBRARY

NOV 1992

CANCELED